A King Production presents...

Power

NO ONE MAN SHOULD HAVE ALL THAT POWER...BUT THERE WERE TWO

JOY DEJA KING

This novel is a work of fiction. Any references to real people, events, establishments, or locales are intended only to give the fiction a sense of reality and authenticity. Other names, characters, and incidents occurring in the work are either the product of the author's imagination or are used fictitiously, as those fictionalized events and incidents that involve real persons. Any character that happens to share the name of a person who is an acquaintance of the author, past or present, is purely coincidental and is in no way intended to be an actual account involving that person.

ISBN 13:978-0986004575
ISBN 10: 098600457X
Cover concept by Joy Deja King
Cover layout and graphic design by www.MarionDesigns.com

Library of Congress Cataloging-in-Publication Data;
A King Production
Power/by Joy Deja King
For complete Library of Congress Copyright info visit;
www.joydejaking.com
Twitter @joydejaking

A King Production
P.O. Box 912, Collierville, TN 38027

This Book is Dedicated To My:

Family, Readers and Supporters.
I LOVE you guys so much. Please believe that!!

-- Joy Deja King

"A thug changes, and love changes, and best friends become strangers…"

–Nas

Chapter 1
UNDERGROUND KING

Alex stepped into his attorney's office to discuss what was always his number one priority...business. When he sat down their eyes locked and there was complete silence for the first few seconds. This was Alex's way of setting the tone of the meeting. His silence spoke volumes. This might've been his attorney's office but he was the head nigga in charge and nothing got started until he decided it was time to speak. Alex felt this approach was necessary. You see, after all these years of them doing business, attorney George Lofton still wasn't used to dealing with a man like Alex; a dirt-poor kid who could've easily died in the projects he was born in, but instead had made millions. It wasn't done the ski mask way but it was still illegal.

They'd first met when Alex was a sixteen-year-old kid growing up in TechWood Homes, a housing project in Atlanta. Alex and his best friend, Deion, had been arrested because the principal found 32 crack vials in Alex's book bag. Another kid had tipped the principal off and the principal subsequently called the police. Alex and Deion were arrested and suspended from school. His mother called George, who had the charges against them dismissed, and they were allowed to go back to school. But that wasn't the last time he would use George. He was arrested at twenty-two for attempted murder, and for trafficking cocaine a year later. Alex was acquitted on both charges. George Lofton later became known as the best trial attorney in Atlanta, but Alex had also become the best at what he did. And since it was Alex's money that kept Mr. Lofton in designer suits, million dollar homes and foreign cars, he believed he called the shots, and dared his attorney to tell him otherwise.

Alex noticed that what seemed like a long period of silence made Mr. Lofton feel uncomfortable, which he liked. Out of habit, in order to camouflage the discomfort, his attorney always kept bottled water within arm's reach. He would cough, take a swig, and lean back in his chair, raising his eyebrows a little, trying to give a look of certainty, though he wasn't completely confident at all in Alex's presence. The reason was because Alex did what many had thought would be impossible, especially men like George Lofton. He had gone from a knucklehead, low-level drug dealer to an underground king and an unstoppable respected criminal boss.

Before finally speaking, Alex gave an intense stare into George Lofton's piercing eyes. They were not only the bluest he had ever seen, but also some of the most calculating. The latter is what Alex found so compelling. A calculating attorney working on his behalf could almost guarantee a get out of jail free card for the duration of his criminal career.

"Have you thought over what we briefly discussed the other day?" Alex asked his attorney, finally breaking the silence.

"Yes I have, but I want to make sure I understand you correctly. You want to give me six hundred thousand to represent you or your friend Deion if you are ever arrested and have to stand trial again in the future?"

Alex assumed he had already made himself clear based on their previous conversations and was annoyed by what he now considered a repetitive question. "George, you know I don't like repeating myself. That's exactly what I'm saying. Are we clear?"

"So this is an unofficial retainer."

"Yes, you can call it that."

George stood and closed the blinds then walked over to the door that led to the reception area. He turned the deadbolt so they wouldn't be disturbed. George sat back behind the desk. "You know that if you and your friend Deion are ever on the same case that I can't represent the both of you."

"I know that."

"So what do you propose I do if that was ever to happen?"

"You would get him the next best attorney in Atlanta," Alex said without hesitation. Deion was Alex's best friend—had been since the first grade. They were now business partners, but the core of their bond was built on that friendship, and because of that Alex would always look out for Deion's best interest.

"That's all I need to know."

Alex clasped his hands and stared at the ceiling for a moment, thinking that maybe it was a bad idea bringing the money to George. Maybe he should have just put it somewhere safe only known to him and his mom. He quickly dismissed his concerns.

"Okay. Where's the money?" Alex presented George with two leather briefcases. He opened the first one and was glad to see that it was all hundred-dollar bills. When he closed the briefcase he asked, "There is no need to count this is there?"

"You can count it if you want, but it's all there."

George took another swig of water. The cash made him nervous. He planned to take it directly to one of his bank safe deposit boxes. The two men stood. Alex was a foot taller than George; he had flawless mahogany skin, a deep brown with a bit of a red tint, broad shoulders, very large hands, and a goatee. He was a man's man. With such a powerful physical appearance, Alex kept his style very low-key. His only display of wealth was a pricey diamond watch that his best friend and partner Deion had bought him for his birthday.

"I'll take good care of this, and you," his attorney said, extending his hand to Alex.

"With this type of money, I know you will," Alex stated without flinching. Alex gave one last lingering stare into his attorney's piercing eyes. "We do have a clear understanding...correct?"

"Of course. I've never let you down and I never will. That, I promise you." The men shook hands and

Alex made his exit with the same coolness as his entrance.

With Alex embarking on a new, potentially dangerous business venture, he wanted to make sure that he had all his bases covered. The higher up he seemed to go on the totem pole, the costlier his problems became. But Alex welcomed new challenges because he had no intention of ever being a nickel and dime nigga again.

Chapter 2
MONEY OVER BULLSHIT

When Alex arrived at the Westin Hotel on 210 Peachtree Street, his main objective was to get in and get the fuck out. Deion was already there when he entered the suite, so Alex figured he would be able to wrap this shit up even quicker than he originally thought. He sat down next to Deion on the couch. They were meeting with John Dixon, who went by the nickname J.D. J.D. was a Tennessee nigga that Alex had been doing business with for the last six years. He was a tall, burly man with a slight mustache, a baby face and was as black as the street. The highlight of his appearance were the gold fronts he proudly wore that said Killa.

J.D. had been a consistent and profitable buyer for Alex over the years, but unfortunately, dealing with him came with one major annoyance. His breath kept a disgusting onion scent that both Alex and Deion detested, and it seemed that there wasn't a mint or a piece of gum strong enough to make the foul odor go away.

"Here you go," J.D. boasted, dumping a suitcase full of cash on the hotel bed. Alex and Deion each scooped a stack and began counting. The two men had a unique relationship. They were business partners, but Alex was the one with the Mexican connection while Deion was the muscle. But don't get it twisted; Alex wasn't the nigga to fuck with because his fist could be just as deadly as any weapon. Deion just preferred to handle any problems that came from dealing with dudes in this treacherous game. Truth be told, he got a sick thrill from murking niggas, whereas Alex only preferred to use violence as a last resort.

"As always, everything is looking good," Alex nodded, picking up another stack.

"Why don't you gimme a break on the price this time?" J.D. slid the request in while Alex was counting up the paper he had delivered on, since he felt Alex was in a good mood.

Alex paused in the middle of counting and eyed him. "J.D., come on man. You know how it is right now. The border is tight and prices are high."

"You expect me to believe you bringing this shit across the border? You right here in Atlanta," J.D. frowned, clearly not sold on what Alex was saying.

"Somebody has to get this shit across the border. It ain't walking itself."

Deion continued to count while listening to J.D. plead his weak case to Alex. Between J.D.'s sloppy-ass huffing even though he hadn't done anything strenuous and his breath stinking, Deion was ready for this meeting to be over with. But making sure each one hundred dollar bill was accounted for made Deion willing to deal with the foul odor and the bullshit coming from J.D.'s mouth.

"But you said it yourself. I'm your best customer. Come on, Alex, man. Give me a break, homie," complained J.D.

"I said you were *one* of my best customers," Alex clarified.

"Listen," J.D. sulked, "I got jammed up and I didn't rat on you—that should count for something."

Deion stopped counting and turned to J.D. "Lemme get this straight—you deserve a break for not snitching?"

"I didn't mean it like that, but just knock twenty-five dollars off the ticket and I'll be grateful."

"Bruh, you gettin' fifteen hundred a pound. That's a five hundred dollar profit on each one of these."

J.D. looked back at Alex and barked, "I can't keep paying these ridiculous-ass prices for this shit!"

"Calm down, I'll give you a twenty-five dollar break on half of them." Relief instantly came over J.D's face.

"The money is all there. You know I'm always good." J.D. said before glancing at his watch. "I gotta get outta here. You know I stay makin' moves," J.D. stated as he headed towards the door.

Alex trusted J.D. He knew that if the money was short, J.D. would be good for it. "Just pack the money back up in the suitcase, we'll count it later." Alex and Deion waited a few minutes after J.D. left, then made their departure. They took the elevator to the lobby where they exited into the parking lot.

J.D.'s black Harley Davidson pickup truck was in the back of the hotel parked on a corner by itself. He hopped in the car and fired up the engine. Seconds later, a man named Reggie drove up in a red Dodge Ram and pulled alongside carrying 5 boxes of weed in the back of the truck. He tossed the boxes in the back of the pickup, secured the tailgate, and

J.D. drove off.

Later that night when Alex and Deion got back to Deion's condo they counted up J.D.'s money. "One thing about that damn J.D.—his money is always right," Deion commented.

"Yeah it is. He do good business, but..." Alex paused and sat down on the sofa, crossing his arms behind his neck.

"But what?" Deion questioned, tossing a stack of money down on the table.

"That comment he made about gettin' jammed up ain't sittin' right wit' me."

"At first I felt some type of way 'bout that shit too, but because he came clean I felt we had nothing to worry about. If he had hid the shit, then I might be concerned."

"True. I just don't want us caught up in no bullshit. The next few times J.D. makes a buy, we gon' switch shit up a lil' bit. It's better to be cautious. I don't give a damn how right the money always be."

Chapter 3
PAY WHAT YOU OWE

A little bad-ass kid named Day-Day stood in front of the apartment building and chomped away at some cotton candy. Most kids were in school, but not Day-Day; he'd been suspended for feeling some little girl's butt in class. It was the third girl he'd felt up before the principal finally suspended his ass. Even at the young age of nine years old, Day-Day seemed destined for a stint in the penitentiary.

"Hey lil' man you know where Tee lives?" Deion asked Day-Day as he and Reggie approached. Day-Day licked his fingers and stared at Deion, looking him up and down before answering.

"It depends."

"Depends on what?" Deion asked.

"Depends on who wants to know."

"I wanna know," Deion said, a little put off by the kid.

"You the police?"

"Do I look like the police?"

"Hell yeah!" Day-Day laughed.

Reggie and Deion stared at each other before laughing, then Deion said, "Look lil' man, tell us where Tee lives and I will give you some more cotton candy."

"Do I look like I want some more damn candy?" Day-Day popped.

Deion pulled out a ten-dollar bill and passed it to Day-Day. The boy closed his bag of cotton candy and tucked the bill in his pocket. Then he turned to Reggie and asked, "Where's yours?"

"Lil nigga, you tryna hustle us?"

"I'm gonna count to five and if you don't give me at least ten dollars, I ain't telling ya'll shit."

"Stop cursing," Deion demanded before Reggie pulled out a ten-dollar bill and passed it to Day-Day.

"Tee lives in 211, bitches," Day-Day grinned and ran off.

Deion and Reggie shook their heads in dismay as they made their way to 211. They knocked on the door for a few seconds. A minute later a pretty young girl answered the door. Before she could say anything, a boney old woman with a grey Afro came running up behind her.

"We looking for Tee," Deion informed them.

"I'm Tee," the old woman announced.

"You not who we are looking for." Deion stated, matter-of-factly.

"I'm the only Tee that lives here. There ain't nobody here name Tee but me."

"There ain't no men in this house?" Reggie questioned before pushing the old woman inside the house and brandishing a gun. Before allowing either of them to answer he continued, "Well then you won't mind if we look around for this motherfucker?"

"Don't kill us," the pretty young girl screamed out.

Deion pulled his gun out and fired a shot into the ceiling. "Would you shut the fuck up!"

The girl calmed down as she stood next to the old woman. "What do you want from us?"

"Where is Terrence?"

"Huh?"

Reggie heard some rumblings and disappeared into the back room. He kicked the door in and saw Terrence prying open a window to make an escape. He had one foot out when Reggie fired a shot that grazed Terrence's ass.

"Fuck!" Terrence hollered as the window smashed the tip of his finger. Reggie leaped towards him and kicked Terrance in the same ass cheek where he'd fired the shot.

Deion heard all the commotion and led the two women into the back room at gunpoint. When they reached the bedroom, Deion barked, "Sit yawl's asses on the bed and don't move."

"Okay, but please don't hurt us," the girl cried out.

Terrence was lying on the floor in the fetal position with his ass still burning from the hot bullet. Deion used his fresh out the box Nike and pressed Terrence's face to the floor. "Where the hell is my motherfuckin' money, Terrence?"

"Look, Deion man, I don't have it. I ain't got shit. If I had it man, you can get it."

Deion kicked him in the face. "I need some collateral."

"I saw this clown nigga riding a motorcycle a few days ago," Reggie said, then gave a sarcastic laugh.

"Where's the bike?" Deion wanted to know.

"That's my son's bike," the old woman said.

"I don't give a fuck whose bike it is. It's my bike now."

The woman started to say something but Deion slapped the shit out of her. "Why in the fuck did you lie to me anyway? How did you know to lie?"

She was lying back on the bed holding her jaw. Reggie aimed the gun continuing to taunt the old woman. "You heard him. Why did you lie?"

"Please don't shoot. We heard y'all out there talking to Day-Day, asking about Tee. That's the only reason we lied," the young girl admitted between sniffles.

"I need for you to stand up," Deion directed. "Do you have a man?"

Tee was still lying on the floor groaning. He muttered, "That's my lady."

"You shut the fuck up!" Deion demanded, before turning his attention back to the girl. "What's your name, young lady?"

"Trina."

"Kind of a plain-ass name for such a beautiful bitch," Deion commented rudely. Trina was a rich brown color and her hair was in two long braids like Pocahontas. Deion had Reggie take the old woman out of the room. Reggie yanked the old woman by the hair and led her out bound with plexicuffs.

"Please don't do nothing to my girl," Tee begged. His ass was leaking and he was in excruciating pain.

"Where is my bread?" Deion asked again, ignoring his pleas.

"Give me a week and I'll give it to you. I promise."

"Promises...promises," Deion taunted, yanking Trina by one of her braids.

"Please don't hurt me." A river of tears rolled down her cheek.

"This ain't about you. This is about your bitch-ass nigga boyfriend. He owe me and now he's gonna pay." Deion pulled out a knife from his back pocket and with ease and precision he let the sharp blade rip open Trina's smooth skin. Blood gushed out of the right cheek of her face. The girl was silent for a few moments as if paralyzed in shock. Once the realization kicked in, an ear-piercing scream soared through the entire apartment, causing Reggie to rush inside the room.

"Deion, what the fuck did you do?" Reggie barked, noticing all the blood gushing from Trina's face.

Deion looked at Reggie for brief moment before answering. "This is payback," Deion said calmly.

"Man, this some bullshit!" Deion ignored Reggie and focused his attention on Tee, who was now in tears. He then turned towards Trina, who had both hands covering her face as the blood continued to flow through her fingers. She shook hysterically, clearly in pain and still in shock. But Deion felt no remorse. In all actuality the money Terrance owed was peanuts to him, but Deion didn't give a damn. There was a code of the streets that he expected everybody to follow when it came to business. If Deion gave one nigga a pass then all of them would start thinking they could slide too, and he had no intentions of entertaining that bullshit.

"Now we're even," Deion stated, stepping on Terrance's face before blasting him in the other ass cheek.

Chapter 4
TUNNEL VISION

"You about to fuck everything up with your bullshit," Alex scolded as he paced in his kitchen. Deion twirled around on the barstool, not really wanting to listen to what Alex had to say. Deion was a grown man so lectures weren't his thing. He had a strong urge to tell Alex to shut the fuck up, but he knew what Alex was saying was on point.

"I'm telling you, man, this is the kind of shit that can get you sent away for a long time," Alex warned Deion, hoping to reach him with reason. Deion turned away, not wanting to make eye contact with his partner and friend. "Are you listening to me?" The tension was quickly building between the two men.

Deion stopped twirling on the barstool and

stared at Alex for a second before speaking. "All he had to do was pay me my fuckin' money, simple as that. We wouldn't be having these issues if that nigga would've handled his business."

"Okay, money is one thing but why did you have to slice his girl's face?" Deion was silent. "You can't tell me slicing his girl is about the money."

Deion stood up from the barstool, but his eyes were still locked on Alex. He walked towards him and as he approached they were now almost nose-to-nose, because Deion was slightly shorter than his friend. "You're right. Fuckin' up his girl's face wasn't about the money."

"Okay, if it wasn't about the money, then what?"

"Principle. It's about motherfuckin' principles."

"So slicing up a woman for no reason represents principles? You need to explain that to me, 'cause I'm lost."

"You know what, Alex? You too soft. Sometimes it starts out with a motherfucker owing you ten thousand then a hundred thousand then more than that. Next thing you know, you working for *that* motherfucker."

"You fuckin' up, homie." Alex paced, then turned to Deion. "So what happens when she files charges against you for assault with a deadly weapon? Then what are you going to do? Will you still think that principle bullshit you spittin' was worth it?"

"It's not gonna happen."

"Oh, you know that for sure?" Deion was quiet again. Although he tried to sound confident in his response, he knew Alex was right; he didn't know that for sure.

"And why the fuck is you selling coke anyway?"

"Why not?"

"Because I'm not trying to get indicted over your fuck ups! I told you we was gon' fall back on the coke for a minute until we know for sure our shit ain't hot."

"What I do don't have shit to do wit' you."

"Really, nigga? See that's where you wrong. It has everything to do with me; we partners."

"I would like to think of it like that, but the fact of the matter is, you have more than I do."

"And who fault is that? It's your lifestyle. Wasting money on every pretty bitch in Atlanta and the strippers too. You also have to be the first to buy the new body style before the shit hit the streets. I mean fuck, you can only drive one car at a time."

"It's my money. I can spend it the way I choose."

"True, but don't act like the paper in this partnership is lopsided just because you choose to throw money away and I don't," Alex shook his head as he stood on the spacious balcony, taking in the Buckhead & Midtown views. "The bottom line is, I'm not tryna win at this drug game just to end up losing anyway and get locked up 'cause you can't keep yo' temper in check."

"Nothing is gonna happen to me and nothing is gonna happen to you."

"Look, man. These real estate investments are gonna make us look legit. At least legit on paper." Alex's face became serious. "If we don't get locked up first."

"Quit saying that."

"Then you quit doing dumb shit. If things go my way, by this time next year we won't even have to touch any type of drug if we don't want to."

Deion grinned and thought of the day he would be legit. Hustling was the only thing he'd ever thought he could do. He was envious of anybody that had made his or her money legit. Deion put his elbows on the counter, nodding his head and believing for the first time that the thought could actually become a reality.

"You heard from Tierney?" Deion questioned.

"How we jump from discussing you maintaining some self-control so we stay the fuck outta jail, to you asking me about my girlfriend? I guess that's your way of saying you ready to move on from that conversation. But nah, I haven't heard from her."

"Really?"

"Why you sound surprised?"

"I thought the two of you was like this," Deion said, crossing his fingers."

"We cool."

"From what my women telling me, you all are more than cool."

"What's that supposed to mean?"

"They be asking me, 'Why can't you spoil us like Alex do Tierney?'" Deion mocked, imitating one of his many women. "Word from them is you keep Tierney in some new shit."

"What the fuck. I ain't bought Tierney nothing new since her birthday and that was months ago. It's not like I mind buying her shit but I been busy. I haven't had time to spend with her to get her anything new."

"That chick Aimee I fuck wit' said yo' girl been posting all kinds of pics on Instagram, flossin'."

"Like I said, I haven't bought Tierney nothing in months."

"If it ain't you, then it's somebody. You know how this game goes. If he payin' then he fuckin'."

"Maybe so, and that's the exact reason why the only woman I trust is my mother. I don't put nothing past these females."

"But you can't wife yo' mother."

"I already got a wife. I'm married to this money," Alex nodded, rubbing his fingers together. "We took our vows and everything."

"Go 'head, and keep chasing that paper; that leaves more pussy for me," Deion smirked.

"Yeah, nigga. Remember you said that shit next time you start complaining about why my money longer than yours," Alex shot back.

"Isabella Loren is here," the security guard in the lobby of his building said over the phone.

"Send her up," Alex replied.

When Isabella entered Alex's condo, he smiled and gave her a hug. When he let go, he couldn't help but comment on the scent of her perfume. "What perfume are you wearing? I didn't wanna let you go," Alex confessed.

"Not sure, it was a gift from Joaquin. I can find out if you like."

"He takes good care of you," Alex commented, observing Isabella's diamond link bracelet and iced out watch. From her shoe game to a simple black dress, everything about Isabella spoke money, and not new money either. She had that well-marinated money glow.

"He does his best," Isabella smiled.

"You're a good woman. It only makes sense that your husband would want to take good care of you. Where is Joaquin?"

"Back in Cali taking care of business."

"What brings you here?"

"He told me to come talk to you."

"You came all the way out here to talk?"

"Alex, you know we don't do phones and barely send text messages. But let me get straight to the point. Joaquin doesn't want to send anymore weed your way. It's too hard to conceal and the money is not lucrative enough."

"Listen, I understand that weed money ain't coke money and I appreciate Joaquin accommodating me. But like I said before, I wanted to keep my risk low for a minute."

"Is that minute up?" Isabella asked coyly. Alex

didn't say anything because he knew that Isabella was used to counting millions of dollars and her man Joaquin was one of the richest men that he'd ever dealt with. "Alex, aren't you ready to be making a minimum of at least a million dollars a month? How would you like that?"

"No doubt. But honestly, one day I wanna get out of this business for good."

"I like you, Alex. I really do," Isabella smiled in a subtle yet flirtatious way. "That's why I want to help you become wealthy. I want you to be able to spend money without ever being concerned over the price."

"Since I've been trying to fall back a little, the money isn't flowing like I'm used to, but I'm still doing pretty decent for myself."

"The world is bigger than Atlanta, darling."

"I know that, and I won't pretend you haven't piqued my interest. The quicker I can stack all this bread, the quicker I can retire from the game. What did you have in mind?"

"Heroin."

"Oh hell no."

"Why not?"

"It's too dangerous and risky. That shit is a mandatory death sentence for users. Too much for the conscience, you know?"

"My grandfather always told me that in order for somebody to live, somebody must die."

"What is that supposed to mean?"

"I used to ask my grandfather the same question, until I realized that with the natural progression of life, whether you're living right or wrong that death occurs so new life can continue. So regardless if you sell the heroin or somebody else does, if it happens to lead to death, life will go on. So why not profit from it if you can, because if you don't, the next man will."

"Let me think about it."

"What is there to think about? You're going to make three times as much money. Isn't that what you're in this drug game for...to make money? Whether you're selling weed or heroin, there is always a risk when you're partaking in something illegal. You might as well maximize the profit for the risk."

"I can't dispute that point." Isabella dug into her purse and handed him a Ziploc back full of product. "What's this?"

"Three ounces of pure heroin."

"You brought this on the plane? How did it get pass TSA?"

"Alex, I don't fly commercial, and anyway, I didn't fly with it. You know we have runners."

"Oh, yeah. What am I supposed to do with this?"

"Put it on the streets and see what happens."

"What do I have to give you?"

"Nothing. It's my way of proving a point," Isabella smiled. "Just keep the profits. Think of it as an early Christmas present," Isabella grinned, stroking the side of Alex's face.

"I have to give you something. This just wouldn't be right."

"I'm staying at the Four Seasons," Isabella said as she stood up without breaking her stare. Alex wasn't sure before, but now he was positive Isabella's interest in him extended beyond business. He was somewhat flattered, but reluctant at the same time. Isabella was married to his connect, which meant she was off-limits.

"Alex, I made Joaquin into a very wealthy man and if you let me I can do the same for you." She leaned in and kissed him.

"Don't do that," Alex said, stepping back.

"Your loyalty is with Joaquin, right?"

"Exactly."

"What Joaquin doesn't know won't hurt him."

Alex couldn't deny that he was drawn to Isabella. Not only was she beautiful, but she was also about her business and making money. That was an alluring combination for a man like Alex.

"I hear you."

"I have the connections. My family is with the cartel. Joaquin is who he is because of me."

"I get it. That makes your husband a very lucky man."

"I can make you a lucky man too."

"You mean luckier," Alex said with ease.

"Your confidence makes you even more attractive."

"And the fact that you're beautiful and your family is with the cartel makes you even more attractive, but I'll pass. Let's keep this strictly business."

Isabella headed toward the door then stopped before she turned the doorknob. "Remember what I told you. I can make you a very wealthy man. If you play this game right, you can make even more money than Joaquin."

Alex smiled after Isabella closed the door behind her. He respected anybody who knew what they wanted and had no qualms about going after it. Alex then glanced over at the package of heroin

Isabella had given him and thought about all the millions he had the potential of making.

Chapter 5
So Ambitious

When Alex pulled up to meet with Danny Sullivan, he had two things on his mind: Making millions and financial investments. If he followed Isabella's lead, Alex felt he had the first part covered. If Danny Sullivan continued to do what he had been doing, then Alex was feeling pretty confident about his investment opportunities too.

"Always a pleasure," Alex said, shaking Danny's hand after stepping out of his car. Alex smiled to himself, eyeing Danny's attire. On any given day he looked broke as hell, but he was loaded.

Danny was a tall white man with a handlebar mustache. He wore a cowboy hat, jeans and a flannel shirt. Danny was indicted on tax evasion a few years earlier and served eighteen months in prison, where he'd met one of Alex's buddies by the name of Go-Fast, who was doing ten years on a drug charge. Go-Fast had told Alex it would be worth his time to see Danny after he was released.

Danny had been standing beside his pickup truck on an empty lot kicking rocks with his dusty-ass boots when Alex pulled up. After some small talk, Danny jumped right in. That was one thing Alex liked about the older man, he never wasted time and preferred getting straight to the point.

"Alex, it doesn't matter if you give one, two or three million, the return rate is going to be the same. Besides, giving me a lump sum of money right now isn't how you win this game on a long-term basis."

"What do you mean?"

"I realize that giving me a few million at one time seems like a lot to you, but the way you win at life is with residual income. Meaning you need to have something coming in every year. To put it simply, your money needs to be making money."

"I realize that."

"Yeah, but you seem to have a problem with the investment return of ten percent."

"It's a little frustrating to realize all I was going to make was a hundred thousand a year off each million I give you."

"This is not the drug business. Most people would be happy making a hundred thousand a year legally."

"I wanna give you another three million and this way I can make 400,000 a year off my investment."

Danny sighed as if he really didn't want to take more money from Alex. Alex had just given him a million dollars a few weeks ago to invest in the new subdivision. "Where is it?"

"In my car."

"Is it all there? I don't want to have to count all that cash like I had to the last time."

"Yeah, it's all there. It may even be a little more."

"I like you, Alex, and I want you to leave that other business alone. You have a lot of potential and I don't want it to be wasted because you end up behind bars."

"Believe me, I'm trying, but I wasn't born rich, you know."

"I know, but you're smart, and that's what I like about you. But if somebody ever finds out that I'm cleaning this money, we're both getting shipped to the Feds."

"Listen, I know that and believe me, I ain't

trying to go there."

"And I'm not trying to go back," Danny added.

"Let's get the negative shit out of our heads," Alex said before walking to the car to retrieve the money. While making his way back towards Danny, Alex noticed a black guy in a red Porsche Panermera driving past them. He blew his horn and waved at Danny. "Who the fuck is that?" Alex inquired.

"Oh, just the architect. The one that designed the homes."

"I knew he looked familiar," Alex said, staring at the car. The tag said ArkTEK.

"Alex, I don't want you to worry about your money. It's in good hands," Danny reassured Alex, getting back on topic.

"I Googled your ass and did my research," Alex admitted, giving a slight smile. "Net worth of seventy-five million dollars. Pretty damn impressive."

"I try," Danny chuckled.

"Trying has definitely paid off for you. Now I'm trying to get my shit lovely but on a legitimate tip."

"That's what I'm here for. But speaking of getting things lovely, how is that pretty young lady you had with you the last time?" There was an awkward silence between the men and Alex wondered where Tierney was. He hadn't heard or spoken with his on-again, off-again girlfriend for weeks.

"She's good," Alex remarked, not caring to share his concerns with Danny. Business was business, and when it came to Tierney, that was personal.

Tierney Mobley opened the door of her condo with a towel wrapped around her naked body. "What the hell are you doing here? I haven't spoken to you in weeks, but you decide to pop up at my crib unannounced. Why should I be surprised? Typical Alex," Tierney scoffed, blocking the entrance.

"I'm the one that paid for everything inside this crib."

"And...you still haven't told me why you are here. What you doing, an inventory check?" she smacked.

"Can I come inside?" With reluctance, Tierney stepped aside so Alex could enter the condo. She led him to the living room area. She sat on an armchair and he sat on the sofa across from her.

"Talk fast, Alex. I have somewhere to be."

"Who is he?"

"What the hell are you talking about?" Tierney questioned while she applied lotion on her long, shapely legs.

"I know you're seeing somebody. I can just tell."

"What makes you think I'm seeing somebody?" she asked nonchalantly, putting the lotion on the table in front of her.

"Patterns."

"What do you mean by patterns?"

"Your patterns changed. You used to call me every morning on your way to work. Then you stopped calling me."

"Alex, I stopped working, remember?"

"Yeah, and I thought that was strange."

Tierney stood up from the sofa and dropped her towel on the floor. Now naked, Alex stared at her impeccable body. She had just a mouthful of breasts, a tiny waist and an impressive ass. But what Alex loved most was Tierney's dark brown skin that was now glistening from the lotion she'd just applied. If she was trying to remind Alex what he was missing, Tierney had succeeded.

She disappeared into the back room and came

back carrying a pink thong, some baby powder and a pair of jeans. She slipped into the thong and it complimented her enviable complexion. At that moment, Alex would've given almost anything to be inside of her.

"So let me get this straight. It's okay for you to do whatever the hell you wanna do, but when I decide to follow your lead and do what you do, it's a motherfuckin' problem?"

"Not a problem at all, I just want to know the truth."

"What are you talking about, Alex?"

"Are you seeing somebody?"

"What difference does it make? You're not my boyfriend, or are you? I mean, you change our relationship status whenever the fuck you feel like it. I can't keep up with the shit, so I'm just doing me."

"So you are seeing somebody?"

"I didn't say that."

"So what are you saying?"

"I'm saying you're not my boyfriend, so why are you stressing me?"

"I got six years invested in this relationship. I deserve to know the truth."

"Alex, six years of off and on bullshit. Plus, you've made it clear you ain't tryna put a ring on it but you want to regulate me. You can't have it both ways. But call me the dumb one because it took me six years to finally figure that shit out."

"So now you got me all figured out...huh?"

"Yeah, pretty much. You're just like your boy, Deion; both of ya'll players that never want to grow up. I want more than this on and off girlfriend bullshit. I wanna get married and have kids one day. I don't see that happening with you."

Alex tried his best to keep his composure. He hated it when she said this because it was so far from the truth. He did want kids and a family, but he didn't want to be in the drug game when he got married. He wanted to be one hundred percent legit.

"Alex, do you think we'll be married in six months?"

Alex looked away before saying, "No." Though he loved Tierney, he knew she wasn't the woman he wanted to settle down with and marry. Alex wasn't in a rush to settle down and thought Tierney was a good alternative until he found who he thought would be the perfect woman for him. Alex reasoned it was a beneficial arrangement for both of them. Financially he kept her straight, they traveled the world together and whatever she asked for he pretty much gave her. In turn, Alex had a woman that pleased him physically, he enjoyed her company as long as it wasn't for an extended period of time, and she stayed out of his business. Unfortunately for Alex, that was no longer enough for Tierney. He was satisfied with their pretend ideal relationship; she wanted the real thing.

"Then what difference does it make if I'm seeing somebody or not?"

"I just think you owe me the truth."

Tierney slid into her jeans, and the way they gripped her ass made Alex want to take them right back off and bend her over. But he knew that there was no way he was going to get any pussy, judging by her tone.

"So you say you want the truth?"

"I'd like that?" Alex said with a serious look on his face.

"So let me tell you the motherfuckin' truth—all you've done is lie to me."

Alex looked confused. "When did I lie to you?"

"Alex, what's the reason you can't marry me?"

"I've already told you why I can't marry you."

"Don't give me that 'you wanna be out of the game' bullshit. Tell me the truth. I'm not what you want." The conversation had now gone completely left. Tierney called Alex out and he wasn't sure how to react. He knew he had no intention of taking their relationship to the next level, but he didn't want anybody else to have her either.

"That's just what I thought. You don't have to say it. I can just tell."

"Who the fuck is he?"

"Nobody."

"Yeah, right. I heard about all those fuckin' pictures on Instagram you postin' tryna show out. That's cool though."

Tierney didn't respond. She disappeared to the back room and came back wearing a pink Hello Kitty t-shirt and no bra, with her nipples piercing through. Alex was convinced Tierney was purposely trying to get his dick hard knowing he wouldn't get the pussy and that was making him even more pissed off.

"So what if I'm posting pictures on Instagram? Again, what difference does it make what I'm doing?" Tierney asked as she sat back down, crossing her arms.

"Why the fuck you keep repeating the same question? Just answer my fuckin' question. Is the truth that hard for you to give?"

"I'ma need you to leave."

"You fuckin' around. Just like I thought," Alex

gave a slight laugh, trying to suppress his anger.

"In order for me to be fuckin' around, I have to be in a relationship," Tierney shot back. She opened her door for Alex to leave.

"This is going to be the worst mistake of your life. I promise you," he cautioned, before walking out the door.

Chapter 6
GET YOUR MIND RIGHT

"This motherfuckin' Lamborghini, is gon' be the reason you go to jail," Alex stated to Deion. Deion smiled and tossed the keys to the valet, as if paying Alex no mind. "What the fuck are you thinking driving around in this flashy-ass car?"

"Yo, calm down. It's a rental, man. My white homeboy Matt at A-Town Exotic Rentals gave it to me for a good rate," Deion explained as they entered the restaurant. Once inside, the hostess led them to a booth in the back.

"We gotta be smarter than this," Alex said when the waitress left.

"Quit trippin.'"

"This ain't trippin.'"

"Yes it is, and for what? You drive Range

Rovers and Benzes and shit. What do you think we do this for? You think I'm gonna be out here risking my life and not having fun? All motherfuckers need to know is that I'm a legitimate business man."

"The fact that you have to use the word legitimate is gonna let people know yo' ass ain't legit."

"I got this, 'cause soon as my rapper 2Glocks hits big, this drug game is over for me and you."

"You been saying that for the last two years."

"It only takes one hit," Deion informed Alex with confidence.

"And it only takes one drug bust and it's over."

"Don't put that energy in the air, man. We gonna win at this game."

"We can't win being stupid."

"So you want me to take the Lambo back to the rental place?"

"That would be a good start."

"Consider it done, big bruh. No sense in stressin' the small shit. So what did you want to talk about?" Deion questioned, keeping the conversation moving along. Alex passed Deion the heroin under the table. Deion examined it without being detected, then he said, "Coke?"

"Nope. Heroin."

"So you tell me to leave coke alone and you're fuckin' with heroin?"

"Look man, Isabella brought this from California."

"Who?"

"Joaquin's wife."

"The gorgeous bitch with the nice ass?"

"Yep. See if you can get rid of it."

"I can get rid of this with one phone call."

"Really?"

"Dude, I been telling you we needed to get into this." Alex took a swig of his water. He knew if anybody could get rid of heroin, it was Deion. "Can you get anymore is the question."

"Yeah, what do we need?"

"As much as you can get. Just bring me back however much you can and we'll split the profit 50/50."

"Cool, and don't forget...get rid of that Lambo," Alex said, before opening up his menu to figure out what he planned on eating.

A cloud of smoke hovered in the studio in Southwest

Atlanta. A dark-skinned rapper with ashy lips and gold teeth named G-5 sucked the blunt like a vacuum cleaner. He routinely did this every time they smoked in the studio, thus earning him the nickname Hoover. Reggie and Deion looked on as 2Glocks waited for his turn to smoke.

"Hoover, can you pass me the fuckin' blunt? After all, I did pay for this shit and it's expensive as hell," 2Glocks spit.

"You need to get your motherfuckin' money back, homie, cuz this shit ain't even all that good," G-5 retorted, passing him the blunt.

"Just like a greedy nigga after he's done smoked almost the entire blunt, then he want to complain," 2Glocks laughed.

"Seriously, it ain't all that."

"Yo ass probably burnt out," Deion said, adding his two cents.

"I guess so," G-5 said.

"Amigo texted me, said he got some low coke prices," 2Glocks said, changing the subject.

"What's his price?"

"Why would you even risk dealing with somebody else? Besides, you know how Alex feels about fuckin' wit' people outside the circle," Reggie nudged Deion and said.

"Ask him when can we get with him," Deion said, ignoring Reggie. 2Glocks shot him a text back and seconds later his phone was buzzing.

"He wants to see us tonight, says he has ten," 2Glocks informed him.

"The price?" Deion asked again.

"They probably gonna say twenty-five stacks or some high-ass number," G-5 said, after inhaling the haze.

"This ain't good," Reggie said, shaking his head.

"I don't see why not," Deion remarked, wanting Reggie to shut the fuck up.

"You don't know these people," Reggie said, not getting a good feeling about the situation.

"First of all, Alex ain't my daddy. Plus, I need to look out for my dudes. They gotta eat, man," Deion countered.

2Glocks' phone buzzed, "Amigo said ten apiece."

"Those are Texas prices. How the fuck can he do that?" Reggie asked, as he shook his head in disbelief. "From past experience when things seem a little too good to be true they usually are."

"These are Mexicans, nigga. They control the prices," Deion rationalized.

"Yeah and this dude has a warehouse off Old National. I've seen the shit myself," 2Glocks said, vouching for his man.

"So why won't they give you shit?" Reggie wanted to know.

"I ain't got the loot, dude," 2Glocks admitted.

"Well why don't you go pick up the work then?" Reggie suggested.

"I ain't sending nobody my money," Deion said, shutting that idea down.

"He wants to know when can we see him."

"Tomorrow."

"He said it would be better if we came tonight."

"It ain't happening. I said tomorrow," Deion stated, not budging.

"Cool. Tomorrow it is," 2Glocks said, after sending the text and getting a response.

"I still think it's a bad idea," Reggie huffed.

"Luckily for me, what you think doesn't matter," Deion said before continuing his conversation with 2Glocks.

Chapter 7
RUN THIS TOWN

"Damn, this line long as fuck," 2Glocks barked, when they arrived at Club Onyx.

"You know I don't do lines," Deion said, as he made his way to the front of the line with Reggie and 2Glocks right behind him.

"What up, D?" the lady up front taking the money said as she nodded her head to the security guard to let Deion and his people through. A scantily clad waitress was at the door to greet them. As she led them to a table in the VIP section, *Fuck With Me You Know I Got It* was blaring throughout the club. Deion nodded his head to the beat as if he felt the song was speaking specifically about him. When they were seated, he ordered six bottles of champagne.

A pretty girl named Sapphire and another

dancer Deion didn't know approached the table. Sapphire sat on 2Glocks' lap and began to stroke his braids. The other girl's face wasn't anything special but she had a body built for the stripper pole: fake tits and a mule ass. She stood in front of Deion, hands on her hips. "I'm Paris."

"I'm D," he said. He'd never give a stripper his full name.

"What can I do for you?" Paris eyed Deion and then her eyes went to 2Glocks and Reggie. She figured Deion had the money because he was the one paying for the champagne.

"We chillin' right now."

"Are you chilling or I'm just not your type?" Paris wanted to know so she wouldn't waste her time.

"Ma, with an ass like that, you every nigga's type, unless they don't like pussy."

Paris laughed and said, "I didn't ask would you fuck me, I asked would you go out with me?"

"Depends." She smiled when she noticed Reggie and 2Glocks staring at her ass. The lime green G-string brought even more attention to her already massive ass.

"Depends on what?"

"If you a cool chick or not."

"If you saw me at the mall would you holla?"

"Probably not."

"Why is that?"

"I don't holla at bitches. They holla at me. Everybody in the ATL know who I am."

"Really? I've never heard of you."

Deion tuned to Sapphire. "You better tell this chick who I am." Sapphire quickly pulled Paris to the side and schooled her before sending her back over to Deion.

"I wasn't trying to be disrespectful, but I've really never seen you or heard of you," Paris divulged. She pointed to a group of guys on the other side of the club, dressed all in black with GMC on their T-shirts. "Now that Get Money Crew. Those niggas ball out."

Deion looked over at the crew of men throwing money in the air like dummies.

"See the tall dark dude? That's big L. He blew forty stacks in here last night," Sapphire told Deion, like that shit would impress him.

"They're more like the Get Indicted Crew," Deion joked, but was dead-ass serious.

"We don't have to flash," Reggie boasted.

"Is that right?" Paris snapped, seeming unmoved.

"What do you think?" Deion asked, ready to dismiss the stripper.

"I know you cute as fuck," Paris said, sitting down on Deion's lap. He reminded her of Boris Kodjoe and he had paper, so Paris wasn't trying to fuck the situation up. Let me reintroduce myself. I'm Paris," she smiled.

"You know what? You might just work out."

"But I'm not your type, remember?" she said in a flirty tone.

"Not really, but..." Deion was hoping Paris wouldn't keep pressing the issue, but the truth of the matter was Paris wasn't cute. Nice body but not cute, which made her fuckable but not much else.

"Let me dance for you then," she purred when a Yo Gotti song came on.

"Go 'head, give me one dance." Paris frowned. Deion passed her a one hundred dollar bill and said, "Most of these clowns in here make you work hard for a hundred dollars. I only want one dance."

Another girl with some beautiful tits, a petite frame and a nice ass walked passed. Deion stopped Paris and said, "Go and get her. Tell her I want a dance." Paris looked pissed off until Deion handed her another hundred-dollar bill. Paris trotted away and came back holding the girl's hand.

"I'm Passion." Paris stood behind her. She motioned to Deion thanking him for the money and left.

Passion had one of those commercial smiles, with pristine white teeth, and her waist was so small Deion thought his fingers could connect around it. "Can I get a dance from you?" Deion asked.

"Yeah, I'll give you a dance as soon as I come back," Passion promised.

"Where you going?"

She pointed to the GMC crew that Paris had just been talking about. "They're spending the money and I gotta go where the money is. I have a son to support."

Deion moved in close to Passion, "So how much is it gonna cost me to take you out of the spot for the night?"

"I don't think you can afford me, Hon," Passion said, ready to brush him off.

"Some of you chicks workin' tonight is clueless. You obviously don't know who the fuck you talkin' to." Deion removed 50 one hundred dollar bills from his wad of cash.

She laughed and said, "I see you got a couple of stacks." She twirled her hair. Deion found her so damn pretty and he wanted her bad as fuck.

"Five grand right now."

"I can dance for you later if you want but I have to go back over there." She pointed to the other V.I.P. area.

Deion placed five one hundred dollar bills in her palm and maintained eye contact. "This is for your phone number." he said.

"You wanna buy my phone number?"

"Yes."

"It's going to take more than that to get my number."

"You gotta be kiddin' me. The nigga you fuckin' on a regular probably some loser that stay at home all day on PlayStation."

"You think so?" Passion asked, not budging.

"I know how this game goes." Then he placed five hundred more dollars in her hand and said, "What's the number?" Passion spit those ten digits so quickly. Deion punched them in his phone. "Call you later."

Paris approached the table smiling. "I see what your type is."

"You my type," Deion said.

"Am I?"

"Of course you are."

"So how much you gone give me?"

"After the club, call me and let's meet up," he said, giving her his number before heading out. As Deion made his way towards the exit, he stopped for a moment when he noticed Passion gyrating seductively for one of the GMC dudes. He felt some kind of way that she was with that nigga instead of leaving the club with him. Right when he was to keep walking, his eyes locked with the dude Passion was dancing for. He nodded his head at Deion and then started smacking Passion's ass, as if sending Deion a message that he got his bitch. Deion simply nodded his head back at the guy and made a mental notation of dude's face, knowing they would cross paths again.

It was three a.m. and Deion was lying in bed wide awake when his phone rang. "Yo."

"Hey, it's Janay."

"Who?"

"Paris from the club."

Deion sat up on the bed. "What's up, babe?"

"Trying to see you, daddy."

"Come see me then."

"You got something for me?"

"What you want?"

"You can give me what you gave Passion. And I'll take care of you."

"Come to the Luxe Condominiums in Midtown. 222 12th St., Unit 1802." No more than fifteen minutes later, security was calling to inform Deion that Paris had arrived and was on her way up. Deion opened the door naked and wasted no time letting Paris know what he wanted. "Get on your knees."

"Shouldn't you be giving me something first?"

"I'm good for it. Get on your knees."

"I need the money first."

Without saying a word, Deion walked toward his bedroom and Paris was right behind him. There were a few thousands of dollars on the dresser. When Paris noticed the money, she stripped down immediately. Deion pointed to the dresser and said, "Count out a couple of thousand dollars."

Paris was surprised with the amount. She wasn't expecting Deion to pay her that much for sex.

"What's up with your girl?" Deion asked, as he went over to his dresser drawer to get a condom.

"What girl?"

"Passion."

Paris counted 20 one hundred-dollar bills. She put the bills in the pocket of her jeans that were lying on the floor then jumped up on the bed with her knees pulled up to her chin. "I don't really know her like that. I mean we cool, but I don't know much about her except she from Alabama," Paris revealed.

"Really?" he nodded his head.

"And somebody is takin' care of her, perhaps a sugar daddy," Paris continued, putting her hand on her hip.

"How do you know all of that?"

"Instagram tells it all?"

"Instagram?"

"Yeah, you know, the photo sharing app."

"Yeah, I got an account with about 20 followers."

"What's your name? I'll follow you."

"I don't remember it. I don't be on there like that."

"Well my name is ITParis, if you want to follow me."

"Got you," Deion said, sitting down on the bed. He was ready for Paris to suck his dick, so he could then fuck her and get her out of his crib. She placed her lips on his manhood and she could feel him rise in her mouth. Paris was anxious to put in work and earn her two stacks, with the hope this would be the first of many more sex sessions.

Chapter 8
NOTHING IS STOPPING YOU

When Deion and 2Glocks arrived to meet Jose, who lived in a very affluent part of Atlanta, Deion wasn't sure what to expect. Jose had asked 2Glocks to come alone, but Deion let it be known that there was no way in hell he was going to let 2Glocks, or anybody else for that matter, leave with a hundred thousand dollars that belonged to him.

"Please, have a seat," Jose said, after introducing himself. He was a rather tall Mexican and spoke very good English. They shook hands and Jose told Deion to take a seat in the living room while he and 2Glocks discussed business. Deion sat in the living room but had his handgun in his waist. He wanted the business transaction to go smoothly but was prepared for combat, just in case. Deion had no intentions of letting anybody leave this house alive if somebody tried to take his money.

A well-built young Mexican dude with a red headband passed through the living room. Deion noticed how muscular his upper body was, as opposed to his legs. He figured the man had been incarcerated. A huge upper body and bony legs usually meant the person had been on that prison workout plan. Deion placed his hand on his gun that was resting on his waist. He kept his eyes on Muscles. The man smiled and waved before heading back into one of the back rooms. While Jose and 2Glocks were discussing business Deion decided to text Passion.

Deion: *What up*
Passion: *Hey*
Deion: *Do you know who this is?*
Passion: *I don't.*
Deion: *You sold me your phone number.*
Passion: *Oh what's up boo. :-)*
Deion: *You act like you happy to hear from me.*
Passion: *Maybe just a lil, LOL*

Deion thought this chick had way too much game. There was no way she could be happy to hear from him. They'd barely spoken last night and she wouldn't have remembered him if he hadn't given her the money. But he decided to play along.

Deion: *When we getting together?*

"Jose wants five thousand more dollars," 2Glocks informed Deion when he came in the living room interrupting his text conversation.

"I don't have that on me. I thought you said the price was ten?"

"Well he went up on the price. I guess because we didn't come last night," 2Glocks shrugged.

"That's bullshit. Get nine instead of ten then."

"Cool." 2Glocks nodded, then turned and disappeared back into the kitchen. Deion resumed his text conversation with Passion, refusing to stress over the price bullshit.

Passion: *Maybe we can meet for lunch one day and talk.*
Deion: *Of course babe. When you want to meet?*
Passion: *Well tomorrow or Thursday. I box on Wed.*
Deion: *Box?*
Passion: *Yeah, gotta keep this body tight.*

Deion thought back to that smile and those perfect tits. He was ready to see that ass in reverse, but he played it cool.

Deion: *Just let me know when you ready.*
Passion: *I can see you on Thursday and then you can buy me that handbag you promised me.*
Deion: *I promised you a handbag?*
Passion: *Lol. I got ya didn't I? No you didn't promise me anything but I know you wanna buy me something.*

Deion grinned as he thought how Passion was a typical Atlanta woman—always trying to dig in a man's pockets. But a handbag was nothing to a nigga like him, so he was on some whatever you want shit.

Deion: *Yeah we can go to the Gucci store at Phipps.*
Passion: *I'm a Louis Vuitton girl.*
Deion: *Cool lets meet Thursday. First we can have lunch then do some shopping.*

Right when Deion was wrapping up his text conversation with Passion, 2Glocks came with the work in a pillowcase. "Everything good?" Deion asked, wanting confirmation.

Jose came in right after 2Glocks and extended

his hand to Deion. "I apologize about the mix up on the price. Keep doing business with me and I'll make sure you get the best prices." Muscle man came from the back room and folded his arms. His arms bulged and he didn't say anything, just stared.

"No problem," Deion said, shaking Jose's hand, although he was a little pissed that he hadn't gotten the amount of product he had come for. But Deion would still make a huge profit, and for him that's all that mattered.

Isabella was staying in the Penthouse Suite at the Four Seasons. She opened the door wearing a silk bathrobe that was so short it barely covered her voluptuous ass. She had the front untied so her ample breasts were clearly visible. When Alex stepped inside her room, she reached out her arms to wrap them around his waist, but he wasn't having any of it.

"What's wrong?" Isabella asked when Alex pushed her away.

"Listen," he sighed before continuing. "I thought I made it clear that I want our relationship to be strictly business. If Joaquin finds out he'll kill both of us."

"Nobody is going to kill anybody. I told you, my father is one of the richest drug lords in Mexico. If Joaquin so much as puts a finger on me I will have his entire family murdered."

What Isabella said confused Alex and made him extremely uneasy. She was Joaquin's wife, yet she didn't have a problem saying she would murder his entire family. He sat in a chair across from the bed and sat quietly for a few minutes. He needed to make sense of it all.

"Isabella, tell me why you're doing this? Something isn't adding up."

"If you must know, Joaquin has many, many women. All of them are very young," she said, rolling her eyes. "I'm sick of the disrespect."

"But aren't you still young?"

"I feel young. I'm only thirty-two. I don't know if it's because we've been together for so many years and the excitement has worn off, or he prefers his women to be teenagers," Isabella shrugged. "The point is, his cheating has now become out of control, so now I'm over this marriage."

"Joaquin always seemed like a smart man to me. I don't understand how he could jeopardize losing you."

"He has a seventeen-year-old Colombian girlfriend. He has kids by two other women. Obviously he isn't that smart."

"I see," Alex said, eyeballing Isabella as she lay across the bed. Every curve on her body was perfect and he couldn't grasp why a man would fuck that up just to taste some new pussy.

"Alex, I have my needs too. Do you know what it's like not to be touched in months?"

"Actually I do."

Isabella completely removed her bathrobe, revealing her exquisite body. Alex felt himself rise. He was trying his hardest to fight temptation but Isabella's determination to seduce him was making it difficult.

"My girlfriend broke up with me," Alex revealed, hoping talk of his ex would simmer the sexual tension in the room.

"Replace her. You're young and rich. At this point in your life all women are replaceable except for your mother."

"True, but it's still hard. I think she cheated on me."

"Well if you think she cheated, she probably did. Perception is reality."

"True."

"Let me help you take your mind off of her."

"As beautiful as you are, I can't do this."

"Then let me make my offer a little more tempting. If I mix some business with pleasure maybe it will eliminate your guilt. Besides being able to make love to me, I'll give you four more ounces of pure heroin. Now how can you refuse that?" Isabella said breathlessly, as she eased towards Alex before dropping to her knees. She unzipped his pants and massaged his now rock-hard dick. She then licked the precum from the tip of his penis. He moaned in pleasure and began running his fingers through her long jet-black hair.

Isabella took him deep inside her mouth and the wetness made him want to feel the inside of her walls. As Isabella continued to swallow every inch of his massive tool, she paused and her seductive green eyes locked with his.

"Alex, I want you to cum all over my face or in my mouth...the choice is yours." Alex couldn't believe what he was hearing. He thought about Joaquin, the man who had made him a millionaire. His dick was in his wife's mouth, the ultimate sign of disloyalty. His days were numbered if Joaquin ever found out. But how would he find out? Alex had to make himself believe that in order to hold onto the pleasure that was engulfing his body. As if losing all control, Alex exploded his semen in Isabella's mouth and a loud groaning sound followed.

After swallowing every drop, Isabella smiled as if she was proud of making him succumb to her. Alex found himself even more aroused, but then when he gathered his thoughts, he stood and said, "I can't do this anymore."

Isabella stepped in the bathroom and Alex could hear the water running. She came back out shortly after wiping her mouth with a facecloth. "Why do you look so worried? Joaquin will never find out about this," she said to Alex as he sat on the bed, appearing to be in deep thought. "This will be our secret," she said reassuringly.

"There is no way I would ever want him to find this out. I owe that man my life."

"And he owes me his life. If it wasn't for me he would still be living in Juarez, one of the worst parts of Mexico."

"I'm sure you remind him of that every chance you get."

"More so now than before. Of course it pisses him off, but it hasn't stopped him from fuckin' around, and I'm the one who made him." Tears began rolling down Isabella's cheeks. She tried to appear so cold, calculating and in control. Maybe she really was comprised of all of those traits, but Isabella was also vulnerable and broken because of her husband's infidelity. "I'm going to make you into one of the richest men in Atlanta," she promised, pulling herself together as she wiped away her tears.

"I can't have sex with you."

"You don't have to Alex, unless you decide you want to. I like you. I can tell you're a good person and you have a conscience. In this business that's extremely rare. So I'm going to take great pleasure in helping you see all of your financial dreams come true."

Chapter 9
MOMENT OF CLARITY

Alex couldn't take his eyes off his iPhone. He continued to read Tierney's text message over and over again.

I think it is best we don't communicate anymore. We're not right for each other and I would appreciate it if you don't contact me since we can't ever talk to each other like two adults. Hopefully one day we can be friends, but right now I don't see it. You have become more of a distraction than a boyfriend.

Alex didn't know how to respond. He was surprised that Tierney had the nerve to completely cut him off via text. He was pacing the floor, wondering how they had reached this point. He had known the relationship was finished a long time ago but he thought they were better than this. Alex knew he hadn't been the best boyfriend in terms of giving Tierney the commitment she craved, but he had treated her good financially and now he felt like she was being ungrateful. He felt a deep anger brewing. *The audacity of this bitch cutting me off by sending me some fucked up text. I was the best thing that ever happened to her and this is how she ends things*, Alex thought as he shook his head. He stopped pacing, sat down on the barstool and dialed Tierney's number. There was no answer. He called again. She didn't pick up, so he sent her a text:

Look, I know you said you wanted to cut off communication, but after all we have been through together at least we can talk this out. Breakup over text...who the fuck does that to somebody they cared about?

Seconds later Tierney texted him back:

Alex, what is there to talk about? I want something that you don't want. I want to get married. You made it clear that you didn't want to get married, at least not to me.

Alex dialed her number again. "What do you want?" Tierney asked when she answered.

"I want to talk?"

"About what?"

"About us."

"We talked about us the other day. There is no us."

"Who is he?"

"Alex, there is nothing to talk about."

"Who is he?"

"I'm so sick of you asking me that same damn question."

"Let's meet face to face."

"We were face to face the other day, and by the way Alex, don't come over here anymore."

"Why?"

"Because we aren't together."

Alex stood and walked over to the vast window in his condo that looked out over the city of Atlanta. He knew Tierney's new man was out there somewhere. He also knew that her new man was holding her down because she hadn't asked him for nada in the last few months. As much as Alex hated to admit it, that pissed him the fuck off. He hated that Tierney no longer needed him for shit.

"So all the time we spent together don't mean shit to you I guess." She was silent. "You never loved me?"

"I've always loved you. Always will."

"What part of love is this?"

"Alex, I loved you."

"Loved? As in past tense?" Those words stung. Although he never planned to marry Tierney, he didn't want her totally out of his life. She represented a sense of comfort for him.

"I was in love with you and I loved you. That will never change."

"But there is somebody else isn't there?"

There was a long pause, "Yes," she finally admitted.

"Who is he?"

"Alex, I gotta go." Tierney ended the call and Alex called her right back but got no answer. He walked back into the kitchen and re-read the text message. Alex felt powerless to Tierney and to the new man. He didn't like this feeling. The thing was, he wasn't sure if the hurt stemmed from his ego being bruised or if it was because he loved Tierney.

The sound of the security desk calling shook Alex out of his dismal thoughts. There had to be somebody downstairs and he hoped it was Tierney, but he knew that was simply wishful thinking. "Hello?"

"Hey Alex, Reggie is here to see you," Joe the security guard said.

"Send him up." Alex tried to pull himself together the best he could before Reggie came up, but he didn't do a very good job.

"What's up, Nigga? You look sad, like you lost your best friend," were the first words out of Reggie's mouth when Alex opened the door.

"I'm good." Alex lied, inviting Reggie in, wanting to deflect from his solemn mood. "So what's up?"

"Just letting you know Deion is fucking up and fucking up bad."

"What that nigga do now?"

"He's dealing with some Mexicans off Old National. He bought some coke from them a couple of days ago?"

"What Mexicans?"

"Some people that 2Glocks introduced him to."

"He just met them?"

"Yeah."

"This nigga here...I can't believe this dude," Alex said, rubbing his chin.

"I know."

"I'll call him."

"No."

"Why not?"

"He'll know that I told you."

"I don't give a damn if he knows or not. I can't be part of somebody else's drug conspiracy."

"I don't see how him dealing with somebody else can hurt you."

Alex stood and walked over to the refrigerator for a small bottle of lime PowerAde. Reggie's eyes were on the bottle, so Alex tossed him one. "If you really thought that, you wouldn't have felt the need to tell me what the fuck he was doing. We don't know nothing about those Mexicans; this ain't good."

"You right, but I really don't want Deion to know that I told you about this."

"I get that, but this is bigger than your need to stay anonymous, Reggie. I sell drugs, but I'm not a drug dealer."

"What is that supposed to mean?"

"It means my life is greater than this. I'm playing this game to win. Not to lose. This is just a means to an end."

Reggie admired how smart and shrewd Alex was. Though he didn't know exactly what his comment meant, he liked the conviction he said it with.

"I want a family one day. Not a baby mama, but a wife and a kid," Alex said wholeheartedly. "And when that happens, I'm gonna be out of this shit for good."

"Okay, I understand."

"So then you understand why I must confront Deion now before this shit get out of hand?"

"Yes, but if there is any way that you can leave my name out of it?"

"Don't worry, I won't mention your name."

"But he's gonna know that I told you."

"Listen, I got this," Alex reassured Reggie as he walked him to the door and let him out. Alex then made his way over to the window that had a sweeping view of Midtown. He stared out as he tried to call Tierney once again, but there was no answer.

"Damn this She-crab soup is delicious," Deion said, as he ate the last bite. He loved the soup at Nordstrom's, which is one reason he'd decided to meet Passion at the Cafe inside the Department store.

"Don't lick the bowl," Passion said, laughing.

"I know what I wanna lick," Deion remarked jokingly, while staring at Passion. She wore a low-cut fuchsia blouse with a white designer scarf that gave her the right hint of sophistication mixed with sex appeal. The slight trace of lip gloss only added to her allure. Deion remembered she was gorgeous but he didn't think she was this damn gorgeous.

"I thought you were going to be on your best behavior," she smiled.

"You right. But seriously, if you weren't here, I might have licked the bowl. That's how good this soup is."

"Don't change things up because I'm here. Do what you normally do."

"Since we're supposed to be doing shit normally, you barely ate anything, just nibbled on a salad."

"I'm trying to lose weight."

"And if you lose that ass, lose my number."

"Oh, all I am is an ass to you?"

"Let's not forget the thighs, tits, and lips." Passion looked annoyed by the words coming out of Deion's mouth. "Come on, girl, you know I'm just kiddin' wit' you."

"Whatever."

"So what the hell is your real name?"

"It's Passion."

"Quit playin' wit' me, you know damn well your mom didn't name you Passion. Passion removed her wallet then presented her driver license: It read Passion Morgan.

"Damn! Yo' mother set you up to shake yo' ass at the strip clubs."

"Well I wouldn't call it a setup," she giggled, "but when I had to drop out of Georgia State, I needed to make money some kind of way."

"I ain't mad at you. We all gotta eat."

"And what is it that you do, D? And what the hell does the D stand for?"

"DeMarcus," he lied.

"Why are you lying?"

"I'm not lying."

"Let me see your license."

"Okay I'm lying."

"Why you lying?"

"My name is Deion."

"Why did you lie in the first place?"

"Well, it's because I don't know you yet. That's all."

"Well you know my name. You're too good to give a stripper your name I guess."

"No."

"So what is it that you do, Deion?"

"I manage a couple of rappers and I have my own label."

"You and every other hustler in Atlanta."

"I don't hustle."

"Hustle is not a bad word and it doesn't have to be an illegal hustle. That's where people get it wrong."

"That's true." He flagged the waitress and ordered another bowl of the She-crab soup. "So when are you going to be my girlfriend?" Deion asked, after his soup came.

"How is that gonna benefit me?"

"So you have to be benefiting in order to be my girlfriend?" Deion questioned.

"Well, a girl needs help every now and then. I have a son to support. I told you that."

"I understand that."

"So what we gonna do about this?"

"Basically you looking for an arrangement?"

"I wouldn't call it that, but I'm just saying, how is this gonna benefit me personally?"

"Come to New York with me next weekend," Deion said, dropping his spoon on the table.

"Invite me." She took a swig of her water.

He stared at her face and realized her eyes

were the color of emeralds. Why didn't he notice that before? Maybe they were contacts, he thought. "I'm inviting you now," he said, getting his thoughts back on topic. Before he could get her response his cellphone rang so he excused himself and stepped outside the cafe before answering.

"Hey motherfucker! That money you gave me was counterfeit."

"Who is this?"

"Paris."

"Who the fuck is Paris?"

"Nigga, you wanna play dumb now! You know damn well who I am!"

"From Onyx?"

"Damn straight from Onyx, nigga. You gave me counterfeit money."

"Why don't you quit lying," he stated, wanting to get her the fuck off his phone.

"I ain't gotta lie about a crummy-ass two thousand dollars."

"Bitch, don't call my phone no more." He hung up and stepped back inside the café. He flagged down the waitress, paid her, then grabbed Passion and left the restaurant.

"I enjoyed myself," Passion said when they got outside.

"Then I know you'll have a good time if you come to New York with me," Deion said, giving her a hug.

"Maybe, but what about my bag?"

"We'll get you one in New York."

"I'm going to hold you to it."

"You good." He handed her five hundred dollars. "This is for your son," he said.

"You're making a believer out of me." Passion folded the money and smiled.

"Keep fuckin' wit' me and won't nobody be able to shake yo' faith. You'll believe in me so much that whatever I say will go."

"I think you a little too confident in yourself but you funny as fuck!"

"And sexy as fuck. Why don't you admit it?"

"Maybe just a little bit," Passion winked, and walked off.

Chapter 10
MONEY OVER BULLSHIT

There was a gray Maserati parked in the driveway of a luxurious home in Gwinnett County. Danny Sullivan had asked Alex to meet him there at 4:45 p.m., but he got there five minutes early. Alex noticed Danny driving up in his pickup truck. He jumped out of his car to greet him. "I thought you would have bought a new car by now," Alex mocked, as the two men shook hands.

"The pickup truck is getting me around just fine. I don't need nothing fancy," he said, nodding his head in the direction of the Maserati. "Hell, I'd have to buy a new wardrobe if I bought a car like that."

Alex looked Danny over—same outfit as last time; jeans, boots, and that country-ass cowboy hat. "You really could use a new wardrobe," Alex suggested, after doing a final inspection on his attire.

"What I got on is fine. Some people spend money on the wrong things," Danny said, brushing Alex's suggestion off.

"So whose car is it? I've seen those custom rims before."

"The architect you saw a few weeks ago at the other property."

Alex had to think back for a second. "Oh yeah, the one with the personalized tags on the red Porsche. I remember meeting him. He said he could design me and Tierney a custom home. Seemed like a nice guy. I still have his card."

"Yeah Milton is a nice man and he's done very well for himself."

"So why did you wanna meet?"

"Well, I wanted to show you this home."

"Why?" Alex inquired.

"Because this is another investment opportunity."

"I've given you as much as I'm going to give you right now," Alex said adamantly. Danny laughed and lit a cigarette. "I didn't know you smoked."

"I don't smoke much. But I'm trying to phase 'em all the way out of my life. Hell, if I don't, they're gonna phase me out of life."

"That's for damn sure." Alex took a step back and fanned the smoke away. Danny dropped the cigarette and stomped it out.

"What I was trying to say was that this is more of a short-term goal."

"Give me the details."

"This house is going to sell for a million dollars, but I happen to know they are about to build a highway in the area and this house will probably be worth 1.5 mil in a year or so."

"A year ain't short-term to me."

"Alex, buy the house, and I swear to you, you'll be able to sell three months after you close for 1.3 million dollars. You'll walk away with three hundred thousand dollars."

"I don't have another million dollars to give you."

"You can finance. Give me a hundred thousand. I'll get you financed for the rest. Once you sell, you'll walk away with a very nice profit."

"Are you sure?"

"Trust me."

"So all I need to give you is a hundred thousand?"

"Yes, and I'll get you a loan."

The architect stepped out of the house and

waved at Danny before jumping into the Maserati. He was a black man that appeared to be in his late thirties or early forties. When he got to the edge of the driveway, he stopped and rolled down the window. "The door is open if you still want to take a look inside."

"Hey, I think I will," Alex replied.

"Great. By the way, how's everything going with you? I remember meeting you awhile back."

"Everything's good. I'm looking forward to seeing what you've done with this place."

"Let me know what you think," the architect said, before speeding off.

"So he designed this house. So far I'm impressed," Alex stated coolly,

"Make that the entire subdivision," Danny stated.

The home resembled a mini castle. What the architect was able to accomplish with his talent made Alex feel proud to be a black man. "Damn, he's good."

"The best in Atlanta. He flies all over the world designing homes for the rich and famous. Just got back from Ireland after designing a chateau for a couple over there."

"That's why he's able to drive a Maserati?"

"Exactly!"

"I'm surprised he remembered me."

"You and your girlfriend must've left an impression."

"Tierney," Alex said under his breath, as a feeling of sadness overcame him for a brief moment.

"Who?"

"Tierney, my ex-girlfriend."

"Sorry to hear the two of you broke up."

"I'm better off without her."

"Are you really better off without her or are you just telling yourself that?"

"Trust me, I'm better off without her."

"You ready to see what you're investing in?"

"Let's do it." When Alex stepped inside the mansion, he instantly knew he would be calling this place home.

Deion was relaxing on his bed when he noticed Passion's name come across his caller ID. "Hello," he answered, actually looking forward to hearing her voice.

"Hey babe, you know you're one funny-ass dude. Was that supposed to be a joke or something?"

"Huh?"

"That money you gave me was fake."

"What are you talkin' about?" he asked, rising up off the bed.

"Deion, you gave me some counterfeit money."

Deion thought about what Paris had said earlier about the money being fake. Now Passion was saying the same thing. He highly doubted them chicks had orchestrated a scam together to try and swindle him, so there had to be some truth to it.

"Are you serious?"

"Dead serious, babe."

"I swear I didn't mean to fuck you, man. Let's meet up later and I will replace the money."

"No worries, you can just give it to me the next time we see each other."

"Thanks for understanding."

"Of course. I'm sure you'll make it up to me in New York...right?"

"No doubt."

When Deion ended the call with Passion he went straight to his closet and pulled out two shopping bags of money. He'd sold the eight that he'd gotten from the Mexicans to a little dude named DeMarco on the West Side. DeMarco's money was in a Neiman Marcus shopping bag. He'd left that bag in the closet because he'd seen Paris before he'd made the purchase from the Mexicans. The other shopping bag was a paper bag from Whole Foods. He'd gotten that money from J.D. It was money he and Alex had divided up the night J.D. was in town. He removed a stack of hundreds from the bag, then went to the kitchen drawer and got a counterfeit pen. He ran the pen over ten one hundred dollar bills.

"What the fuck! I can't believe this shit," Deion said, tossing the bills down. "I know this nigga ain't stupid enough to give us counterfeit money! I thought that motherfucker valued his life." Deion immediately called Alex.

"What's up," Alex said, when he answered.

"We got problems."

"What kind of problems?"

"That funky breath nigga J.D."

"What about J.D.?"

"J.D. ain't right man. I knew we shouldn't have trusted his ass when he wanted a break."

"What the hell are you talking about?"

"Where are you?"

"I'm at home."

"Okay, I'll be there in a few minutes so we can talk face-to-face."

Deion was at Alex's front door so fast he barely had enough time to put some clothes on. "Must be serious for you to rush over like this," Alex said, when he opened the door to let Deion in.

"J.D. has fucked us good!" Deion said, with anger dripping from each word.

"How?"

"The money he gave us was counterfeit."

"Counterfeit?"

Deion tossed a thousand dollars on the table "This is monopoly money!"

"That bitch-ass nigga. You positive it was J.D.?"

"Hell yes!" Remember when I left your house that night? I took a Whole Foods bag."

"Yeah, I gave you that bag. And you didn't put nobody else's money in there?"

"Nope, just that motherfucker's."

Alex went in his bedroom to get the suitcase that J.D. had given him. He hadn't even had a chance to touch the money. Alex pulled a stack of money. All hundreds. He went back into the living where Deion was waiting. He ran the counterfeit marker across the bills.

"See, it's all fake," Deion said through clenched teeth.

Alex dialed J.D.'s number. It was out of service;

it had been disconnected. "What the fuck!" Alex barked before slamming the phone down.

"Thinking back, J.D. had seemed a little off. He just didn't seem quite like himself. But you know what? We slipped too. We normally always have a counterfeit marker with us, but we been doing business with J.D. so long we figured we could trust that nigga. But we both know in this game you not supposed to trust nobody."

Alex dumped the rest of the money on the floor. They unbounded it from the rubber bands. Deion marked it. All fake.

"Three hundred thousand dollars counterfeit," Alex said, as his stomach tightened up from disgust. "So how did you find out about this?"

"A stripper told me I'd given her fake money."

"So you've spent some of yours?"

"Yeah some of it," Deion said, looking away.

"Besides a stripper, what else?"

"I made a move."

"What do you mean you made a move?" He assumed Deion was talking about the Mexicans, but he wanted to wait and see if he would admit it himself.

"I know you told me not to do it, but I did it anyway."

"Did what...bought some coke?"

"Yeah."

Alex took a deep breath and tossed the money back in the suitcase. "I told you not to fuck with that coke," Alex said, not in the mood to welcome the stress that comes with dealing with illegal street shit.

"I know, but the deal was too good to pass up."

"You haven't learned yet that shit that seems too good to pass up be the biggest pile of fuckery." Alex made his way back to the window. He paid extra for this particular unit simply for the views; it was almost like therapy for him to look out and see the city of Atlanta. Tonight Alex felt he needed that healing touch more than ever. Between business and his personal life, it had him feeling some type of way. As he stared out he looked down and could see people wearing shorts and enjoying the summer night. The sky was blood red. He thought about how much Tierney liked red skies, and he wondered where she was. Then he thought about J.D. and where the fuck he was.

"An amazing offer, huh?" Alex questioned, stepping back into reality.

"Texas prices right here in Atlanta."

"Who did you get it from?" Alex turned from

the window and was now facing Deion.

"Mexicans. It was 2Glocks' connection."

"You and your little pissy-ass rapper are gonna fuck everything up."

"What you mean?"

"You don't know these fuckin' Mexicans."

"They're cool."

"You mean cool like J.D.," Alex spit with sarcasm. "How the fuck do you know?"

"Man, listen. I was tryna make what I thought was a good business move. It's easy for you to fall back, you got money!"

"Nigga, you have money too."

"After I gave you the money for the attorney and the real estate investments, I wasn't left with much," Deion complained.

"But you had money. Maybe not as much as you wanted, but you was good."

"You right."

"I was hoping you would invest more money, but it looks like you can't handle it right now."

"Nah, I can't do it. Not now. I just don't have it to give. You know if I did, I would."

"Lets get back to them Mexicans that you don't know."

"What about them?"

"Can't you see what that can lead to?"

"I do." He looked away from Alex.

"I don't believe you do." Alex sat down across from Deion and clasped his hands together. His face oozed of seriousness. "Let's say the Feds are watching the Mexicans and you and 2Glocks walk right into an investigation. Then they are watching you and then they start watching me and even my connect. I've seen this happen time and time again."

It took Deion a moment to respond because he was lost in his thoughts. "Yeah, I know a few dudes that got caught up in on some shit they didn't have anything to do with."

"You have to be more careful." He stood and walked over to Deion and fist bumped him. "Don't get us fucked up."

"I won't, but if I see that bitch-ass J.D. again, I'm killing him. We can't take losses like this. This ain't cool. Not at all."

"Best believe we will see his ass again."

Chapter 11
DIG A HOLE

Joaquin looked like an ordinary white man, but he was Mexican. He had blue eyes and if it wasn't for his dialect, people would assume he was American. He was dressed in expensive jeans, driver shoes and a watch that cost as much as a car. He arrived at Alex's condo in a chauffeur-driven Rolls Royce Phantom. There was a Colombian girl who appeared to be a teenager in the back of the car with him. Alex instantly thought about what Isabella had told him.

"This is Penelope," Joaquin said proudly when Alex approached the car. Alex shook her hand. The girl looked like a younger version of Isabella. Alex led them into his building. They took the elevator to Alex's penthouse and when they were seated Joaquin immediately began to talk business. "I have a plan for us."

"I'm all ears."

"Isabella told you about the new product."

"Yes."

"What did you think?"

"It's risky."

"How?"

"People OD on heroin and die."

"If you're fortunate enough to live then you're unfortunate enough to die...it's called life. So what's your point?" Joaquin was very casual when he spoke of mortality, probably because where he grew up he was surrounded by death on a daily basis so he had become indifferent to it.

"I have a conscience."

"I have one too."

That comment made Alex eye Penelope who hadn't spoken a word. Alex wondered if she could speak English, so he offered her something to drink using a hand motion.

"Agua," she said, confirming Alex's thought that she spoke little-to-no English. Alex came back with a glass of filtered water and handed it to Penelope, who was now sitting on Joaquin's lap.

"If somebody overdoses it'll bring heat," Alex said, feeling uncomfortable watching Isabella's husband sport his side chick in front of him.

"Alex, you don't understand. You are working with an elite group."

"And?" Alex questioned. He was actually about to say something else but he was distracted by Penelope rubbing on Joaquin's chest and giving him small pecks on the jaw. Alex still thought that Isabella was prettier. This girl was just replaceable arm candy. As if reading Alex's mind, Joaquin barked something in Spanish, which brought all that unnecessary foreplay to a halt. Penelope stood up, smiled, walked to the other side of the room and sat on the sofa.

"My lawyers make cases go away."

"This is Georgia. It's a little bit different out here, friend."

"I know about Georgia. Alex, you're not the only one I've been supplying out here."

Alex's eyebrows rose. "Really?"

"I already have a guy out here and he's selling tons of heroin, maybe the biggest heroin dealer in Atlanta."

"So what the hell do you need me for?"

"I want to get rid of him."

"What do you mean?"

"He crossed me, Alex, so he must die," Joaquin

smiled and said, as if the idea of that person dying brought him some sort of pleasure. Alex thought about the night he'd gotten head from Isabella. He knew if Joaquin found out he would die too.

"How did he cross you?"

"He is getting product from a rival cartel. Somebody that I know."

"You're going to kill him for that?"

"I made him into a multimillionaire. For that alone I deserve loyalty."

"But you benefited, too."

"That's not the point. Loyalty is everything to me." Alex couldn't help but think that that same loyalty must not apply to his wife and marriage.

"I understand that, but I'm still uneasy about dealing heroin."

"Over twenty thousand motherfuckers died in Mexico last month. It's part of the business. It's part of fate. When it's your time to go, it's your time to go."

"I'm trying to get out the game, not get into it even deeper. After I make a certain amount of money, I'm done with this."

Joaquin stood and walked over toward Penelope, who was still sitting looking pretty like a baby doll. He kissed her and took a sip of her water. "So what are your goals?" Joaquin asked, turning towards Alex. Alex seemed confused by the question. "What are you looking to make?" Joaquin asked, simplifying his question.

"Well, I guess a few million."

"What's a few million...six or seven?"

"That's a nice number."

"Heroin will help you make at least ten million dollars in the next six months."

Alex thought about it. If he could make ten million dollars in the next six months he could retire from the game, find a wife to start a family with, and keep flipping houses. "Damn, so you really think I can make ten million dollars in the next six months?"

"I can guarantee it. So how much do you think you can handle?"

"What?" He knew what Joaquin was talking about but he was nervous. "How much what?"

"Product." Alex looked over at Penelope; she was nursing her glass of water.

"She doesn't speak English."

"I don't like women in my business."

"That's not true, you speak to my wife all the time."

"True but you all were together when I met you."

"¡Vaya al baño!" Joaquin said to Penelope.

She stood and headed to the restroom like Joaquin had asked. When Alex heard the door shut he felt comfortable enough to discuss numbers.

"I can handle maybe two kilos."

"I want to send you five."

"Why so much?"

"I want you to run this town."

Alex couldn't dispute that. The two men shook hands and then Joaquin shook a little harder before saying, "Death is about to surround us, but we can't worry about that. It's time to get rich. Very rich."

"We have a motherfuckin' problem," Deion said to 2Glocks, as they sat at a corner table during lunchtime at the Pink Pony strip club.

"What type of problem? Shit been lookin' real good from where I'm sittin'," 2Glocks shot back, while eating French fries and sipping on a coke. Deion had water.

"I'm stuck with a shitload of counterfeit money."

"What the fuck? How did that happen?"

"This clown nigga J.D. from Tennessee gave it

to us."

"Does it look real?"

"Not only does it look real, the shit feels real as fuck too. Like a bitch wit' an excellent ass and tit job."

"Word...so then what's the problem?"

"The problem is I took a loss and I think I gave some of it to your connect."

"Really?" 2Glocks questioned, as if unconcerned. He dipped three French fries into a puddle of ketchup. "Ain't nobody said shit to me about it."

"That's strange."

"I'm serious. Nobody has said one word to me." He stuffed the three fries in his mouth and continued, "Well, that's not so strange. Those motherfuckers make so much money. They probably haven't gotten around to counting yours yet. Gotta figure they making millions of dollars."

Deion sipped his water, thinking about J.D. It was ripping Deion's insides up that he had gotten over on them. It seemed like every minute of the day he was visualizing the different ways he was going to slice the motherfucker up when he got a hold of him. That fact was the only thing that was keeping Deion sane. "Eventually they'll find out."

"Maybe, maybe not. By the time they do,

maybe they won't be able to trace it back to you. As a matter of fact, he called me last night and asked if we were ready for more."

"They have more?"

"Yep," 2Glocks said, taking another sip of his Coke. "They have plenty."

"Oh yeah?"

"They heavy in the game. This ain't no hobby or part-time job, them motherfuckers full-time in this shit."

Deion was about to ask 2Glocks a question when a skinny blond girl with no ass and no tits attempted to sit on Deion's lap. He pushed her away. She smiled, revealing a meth mouth before saying, "Somebody is afraid of pussy."

"Naw, I just need you to step. We in the middle of something."

Meth-mouth turned to 2Glocks and said, "Don't tell me you're afraid of pussy too."

"You ain't got no ass," 2Glocks stated, ready for the chick to bounce.

"You need to go to Onyx for ass."

"That's why I'm here for lunch, now scoot," 2Glocks barked, obviously irritated. After the meth-mouth eased away, 2Glocks jumped right back in the conversation. "So what are you going to do with the rest of the counterfeit cash?"

"Probably just throw it away. Haven't really thought about it."

"How much you got?"

"About fifty thousand dollars worth."

"Hell let's take the rest of it to the Mexicans."

"Man, doing shit like that is dangerous. I want no part of that."

"So you gonna just take a loss like that?"

"I'ma get the motherfucker that gave us the bullshit money. But if I can't get the cash back, I just have to chalk it up to the game."

"But in the meantime?"

"Naw, we can't do that." Deion noticed Meth-mouth come running back to the table holding a black girl's hand. She introduced the girl as Chyna. Chyna had a huge ass and an even bigger stomach.

"How is this for a big ass?" Chyna's ass was ginormous with lots of cellulite, and Deion was not turned on in the least. When Chyna smiled, Deion noticed that she was actually pretty cute. Cute little button nose, almost perfect teeth with slanted eyes. Deion dug into his pocket and gave Chyna and Meth-mouth 50 bucks apiece.

Chyna was about to remove her G-string when Deion said, "No, you don't have to dance. Just go away while I talk to my friend."

"So I'm not good enough to dance for you?"

"It's not like that. I'm just in here to talk business," Deion explained, trying to keep his cool but quickly becoming agitated. Chyna and Methmouth finally got the hint and strolled off hand-in-hand to another table.

"Real talk, I need the money. I got kids to feed," 2Glocks said, finishing up his last French fry.

"But that's your plug. Do you really wanna do them like that?"

2Glocks' eyes became serious. "Give me the money, please. Do this for me."

Deion thought about Alex. He was glad Reggie wasn't around, because he knew he would not approve of it, and he was sure that he'd report back to Alex. "I will, but you can't tell nobody."

"Who would I tell?"

"I don't know, but I just want to make sure we're clear that nobody is to know about this shit."

"I appreciate you man. Thanks for looking out."

"Not a problem."

Chapter 12
BEWARE

Popcorn was a burly light-skinned dude with outdated braids. He spoke with Californian lingo because he was originally from L.A. but had lived in Atlanta for the last fifteen years. Deion knew that Popcorn was the man to see about the heroin trade and they were pretty good friends. They'd met when they were both fifteen years old at juvie.

"Come in," Popcorn said when he opened his apartment door, a Newport cigarette dangling from his mouth.

Deion grinned when he saw his friend and they fist-bumped. "This 2Glocks," Deion said, introducing him to Popcorn before following him into the kitchen. Once they were seated at the table, Deion presented him with the two ounces of heroin.

"What you want for this?" Popcorn asked, after examining the product.

"Now you know I don't know much about this game."

"I can give you $5,000 apiece. I'm trusting that this shit hasn't been stepped on too much."

"Probably not at all."

"Bullshit, everybody steps on it. Nothing is pure."

"I got this straight from the Esses."

"I don't give a fuck if you got it from Afghanistan. It's probably been stepped on."

"We don't know how many times it's been cut or if it's been cut."

Popcorn pulled out a baggie with a stamp of a basketball player on it and said, "This is Lebron James."

Deion examined the package and asked, "Why Lebron James?"

"He the motherfuckin' champ, ain't he? Plus, it's easy to remember," Popcorn said, as if he was offended by the question.

"This your shit?"

"You better believe it, and it's the purest shit in the A. It's been cut at least twice."

"Gimme the ten stacks."

"I'll give you that on your word and if it's fire I'll give you more," Popcorn said.

"Cool."

Popcorn disappeared to the back room and came out with 80 one hundred-dollar bills and 100 twenties. He passed the money to Deion. As Deion was doing a quick money count they heard somebody banging at the door. Popcorn picked his cigarette up from the ashtray, eased over to the door and peered through the peep hole. When he opened it a short black ashy dude came in the house.

"Corn, can I talk to you for a minute?" The man looked at Deion and 2Glocks but didn't speak.

"What the fuck you want, Dave? This shit better be important." Popcorn and Dave disappeared to the back room.

2Glocks looked at Deion, "Hope these niggas ain't on no funny shit."

"This dude was like a brother to me in juvie. We don't see each other much, but it's nothing but love between us." With that being said, Deion still pulled out his counterfeit pen and checked those bills to make sure he didn't get got again. He was relieved when everything turned out sweet.

Dave and Popcorn came out of the back room looking like they had just had an intense conversation. "Thanks for the info," Popcorn said, before handing Dave a bag of Lebron James. When Dave left, Popcorn turned to Deion with a stern look on his face. "There some niggas out there beside your car and Dave said they got guns and shit."

"What the fuck? Are you serious?"

Popcorn inhaled on his cigarette, walked to the window and looked down at Deion's pickup truck. There was a black-colored Dodge Charger with two men sitting in it parked beside his truck. "I've seen that car before," Popcorn said.

"Ain't nobody got no issues wit' me." Then he thought about Paris and the counterfeit money he'd given her, but he doubted that bitch would take it this far.

"I don't know," Popcorn said, still looking at the car. One of the goons got out and pissed on the rear of the car.

"That's Travis. We call him Trav," Popcorn said, recognizing one of the guys.

"How you know him?"

"He has a fine-ass sister named Trina. Somebody sliced up her face a few weeks back."

"She got a boyfriend named Tee?" Deion questioned.

"Yeah, how you know?"

"I shot him in the ass."

"So it was you that sliced her up?" Popcorn asked, shaking his head.

"Maybe, maybe not."

"Maybe my ass. Her brother thinks otherwise, and that's why he's babysittin' yo' truck wit' guns ready to shoot."

"So those clowns are waiting on me?"

"Who else you think they waitin' for...damn sure ain't me."

Deion brandished a black nine millimeter. "I swear it will be a shootout in this bitch. I ain't goin' out like that, Corn."

"Slow down, cowboy, I got about sixty thousand dollars worth of heroin in here. Ain't gonna be no shootout in my parking lot."

"I'll respect yo' house, but you know I gotta get the fuck outta here."

"Yeah," Popcorn said, starting to feel a little nervous about the situation. He finished his cigarette then lit another one. "I got an idea."

"Let's hear it."

"I'll walk your man down to the car, let him get in and drive away."

"Then how in the hell am I gonna get outta here?"

"You gonna have to wait it out, big boy," Popcorn said, point-blank.

"What the fuck!"

"Once they gone, I'll take you home."

Popcorn and 2Glocks made their way to Deion's pickup truck. The goons got out of the car.

"What up, Popcorn?" Travis said, giving him a pound.

"Nothing much, just handling some business with my cousin," he said, nodding his head in 2Glocks' direction.

"You know Deion?" Travis questioned, not cracking a smile.

"Yeah, I'm a rapper and Deion my manager, why?"

"I ain't got no beef wit' you, but I need to handle some things wit' Deion. So let him know next time I see him, it's on."

"I don't deliver those type of messages. When he see you I guess he'll know," 2Glocks said before driving off.

Tierney's Instagram account had pictures of intimate dinners, shopping bags, jewelry boxes and fancy restaurants. Alex wasn't a big social media person, but he did use Instagram occasionally, although he only had a handful of followers and three pictures. While skimming through Tierney's pictures, security called informing him Deion was on his way upstairs. Alex welcomed the diversion so he could stop Instagram-stalking Tierney.

"What up," Alex said when he let Deion in. Deion passed Alex the ten grand that Popcorn had given him. "So what did they say about the product?"

"I don't know. My homie, Popcorn, took it because of my word."

"Popcorn, where have I heard that name before?"

"You remember him. The light-skinned dude from L.A., we seen him at the carwash."

"You were at juvie with him or something?"

"Right, that's him." Deion said. He glanced over Alex's shoulder and noticed he was looking at Instagram. "Ain't got over her yet, huh?"

"No, it's not that. Just wanted to see what she's been up too."

"You still love her?"

"I care about her. There is a difference."

"Whatever. Lie to yo'self if you want."

"So Popcorn can help us?" Alex asked,

dismissing what Deion said.

"Heroin is his thing, so he can definitely help us."

"What do we need to do?"

"Once he gets rid of what I just gave him, which shouldn't take him long, we give him more product." There was a silence. Alex was thinking. He knew Deion trusted Popcorn, but he didn't know him. There were enough rats running around Atlanta. He didn't want one in his circle.

"So you sold him the two ounces?"

"Yeah, he had the money at his house."

"So what can he move?"

"He's moving little baggies but he doesn't have access to weight."

"Baggies?"

"Yeah, this shit is much different from the coke game or even the weed game."

"I know that. Pure heroin can be cut at least ten times."

"More than that."

"So how is this dude gonna help us if all he's selling is packets?"

"That's all he has access to."

"I see. Well I'll have five kilos in about a week," Alex informed Deion.

"I'll let him know."

Popcorn had reached out to Deion three times before Deion finally called him back. "I need to talk to you bruh."

"If I come over there and those bitch-ass niggas run up on me this time, it's gonna be bad. Real motherfuckin' ugly, because I ain't hiding."

"We can meet somewhere else, homie," Popcorn laughed. "You tell me where you want to meet."

"Lets meet at Starbucks in Buckhead."

"Starbucks it is," Popcorn chuckled.

"What's funny?"

"Nothing, it's just I've never been asked to meet at Starbucks. I'm just not the latte type of nigga. But it's cool though."

"Okay, I'll meet you there in twenty."

"The one on Peachtree or Piedmont?"

"Piedmont."

Deion sat in the back table beside two geeks pecking away on their Macs, immersed in their work. Popcorn entered the place and scanned it. He didn't look nervous but he damn sure looked out of place.

"Oh, so this is your hangout, huh?" he asked when he sat down across from Deion.

"Somebody got jokes," Deion smiled.

"No, I was just saying I never thought a dude I met in juvie would be hanging out in Starbucks sipping espressos and shit."

"You have to expand your mind, homie, besides I go everywhere, so stop dissin' Starbucks," Deion grinned.

"You over here talkin' 'bout Starbucks but yet you slicing up chicks. I still can't believe you did that."

"Man, quit saying that. I ain't in the mood for no damn lecture. Her nigga should've paid his bill and none of that shit would've happened. Let's move the fuck on. So what did you want?"

Popcorn leaned forward and pulled out a packet of heroin reading *Happy Birthday* and a picture of a birthday cake on display. "Nice...right?" Popcorn had a big Kool Aid grin on his face.

"Put that shit up," Deion snarled. He scanned the coffee shop. The geeks were still pecking on their laptops, not paying attention.

Popcorn put the packet away. "This shit right here is better than Lebron James," Popcorn bragged like he created the shit.

"What? Really?"

"Man, the best shit I have ever ran across," he stressed.

"So you have more money for me?" Deion laughed.

"What?"

"You said if it was purer than we thought, you would give me more money. What, you got amnesia now?"

"I'll give you a couple more thousand."

"I'm just kiddin' wit' you dude. I was only giving you a reminder."

"Can you get more of this?"

"Yes."

"This same exact dope?"

"Pretty sure I can."

"If you can get this, we'll be rich, nigga. I'm talkin' rich as fuck!"

"I can get it."

"When?"

"In a few days."

"How much are you going to have?"

"More than you can handle."

"The reason I asked is cuz I want to be a supplier to other niggas."

"A wholesaler?"

"Wholesaler, supplier, whatever you wanna call it."

One of the geeks stopped typing and asked, "Do you know what time it is?"

"Ain't the time on your computer?" Popcorn popped, giving him the side eye.

"Yeah, I forgot."

"Forgot my ass...Let's go outside," Popcorn said, ready to go.

"Gimme a few days and we'll be in business," Deion confirmed once they were outside. Popcorn got his Kool Aid grin back at the sound of that and they went their separate ways.

Chapter 13
WORLD ABLAZE

Isabella was staying in the same Penthouse Suite in the Four Seasons that she had stayed at before. When she arrived in town the first call she made was to Alex. She wanted to see him, and although he tried to play it ultra cool she could tell he wanted to see her too. When he arrived, unlike before she was fully dressed, yet just as alluring. Isabella was wearing a cobalt blue wrap dress that displayed the right amount of skin to pull a man in but also left something to the imagination. Her strappy open-toed heels elongated her shapely legs. Her jet-black hair was flowing loosely around her tiny accentuated waist.

"Where is Joaquin?" Alex wanted to know as soon as he stepped in her suite.

"I'm not sure where he's staying. He didn't want me to know. He said the less I knew the better off I'd be."

"What did he mean by that?"

"From what I understand somebody Joaquin was supplying heroin to double crossed him. He went behind his back and started dealing with another cartel."

"I think he mentioned that to me."

"I'm sure. He seems to be telling anybody that will listen. It's amazing how important loyalty is to him but he doesn't have any for his wife. But I guess that's how the game goes sometimes."

"And you want me to see you behind his back. I don't think that would be smart."

"How would he find out? I have no intention of telling him."

Alex walked to the other side of the room, grabbed a bottle of water from the dresser and sat at the table. "He said you would have something for me."

"Yes, I do." Isabella made her way over to the closet. Alex was mesmerized by how she moved with so much ease and sexiness, yet sophistication. All he could think of is what a fool Joaquin had to be to let a woman like Isabella slip through his fingers. She removed a shopping bag from the top of the closet and presented it to Alex.

"There are six kilos in here, but you only have to pay for five."

"Huh?"

"I told you Alex, I want you to do well."

"I believe that, but you're also playing with my life."

"Never that. But I can't deny that I want you," Isabella said, reaching out to caress the side of his face. Alex grabbed her wrist, stopping her midair.

"Don't do this," he said with his mouth, but his eyes were saying something entirely different.

"You should stop trying to fight the inevitable. If we don't end up in the bed now, it will happen eventually. So it's up to you if you want to continue to waste time."

"Your husband is in the same city as us right now."

"He doesn't even know where I'm staying and I'm sure he's somewhere with his little fuck-toy."

Alex instantly thought about Penelope, but decided not to entertain that. This wasn't about the other woman in Joaquin's life, it was about his own safety. He had to decide if giving into his undeniable attraction to Isabella was worth the cost. But then again, maybe she was right and there would be no ramifications for their affair.

"Is that what you want from me...to be your fuck toy?"

"I'm a grown woman. I don't do fuck toys."

"So what do you want from me?"

"Right now I want you inside of me. I haven't had sex in months and I need to feel desired by a man that I desire, which is you."

"Why don't you just leave Joaquin then?" Alex probed, before taking a sip of his water.

"It's not that simple."

"Is this the same dope as before?" Alex asked, changing the subject without pushing for a further explanation.

"Why do you ask?"

"Word on the street is that your heroin is on some next level shit."

"And just think, I had to practically shove it down your throat for you to bite," Isabella smiled. Alex stood and grabbed the bag from the table. As he was making his way to the other side of the room, Isabella stepped forward, blocking his movement. He could've gone around her, but he didn't want to. He enjoyed their closeness. He was able to get a whiff of the expensive perfume that she always wore. It seemed to be just as intoxicating as her physical beauty. Isabella licked her lips in a delicate way, letting Alex know that she was all his if he wanted her.

"Lock the door," he directed, as a rush shot through him. He had no intention or even desire to deny their mutual attraction. Alex would no longer put up any resistance. Sometimes playing with fate was truly the ultimate high.

Deion handed 2Glocks fifty grand in counterfeit and then another twenty-five thousand real cash. They counted the money at Deion's dining room table. "It's all there," Deion said.

"Thank you, man."

"No need for that."

"I'm just grateful I can finally do something for my kids."

"I feel you on that, but I just want everything to go according to plan."

"It will. We good, bruh," 2Glocks insisted without hesitation. Without responding, Deion heard his phone ring. It was Popcorn.

"Yo. What's good?"

"We meeting today?"

Deion knew he wanted to know if the product was here. "Probably not today."

"Let me know soon as you can, 'cause I need that."

"Will do." When Deion hung up the phone with Popcorn a text from Passion immediately popped up.

Passion: *Hey Daddy, can I meet up with you to get that money for your son*?

Deion had teased her that her son was his son.

Deion: *Of course baby*.

Passion: *Where*?

Deion: *Waffle House Old National.*

Passion: *What time?*

"What time are we going to meet the Esses?" Deion asked 2Glocks.

"In a couple hours."

Deion scanned his watch. It was four o'clock. He hit Passion back and told her around six. He figured after he finished things up with 2Glocks and the Esses, she would be his very next stop.

Passion sat in a booth inside the Waffle House eating pecan waffles and bacon when Deion and 2Glocks drove up in a yellow Lamborghini. Deion turned the ignition off but left the radio playing to keep 2Glocks occupied. Passion began grinning hard when Deion came in and sat across from her.

"Why the big smile?"

"Because every time I see you I feel like it's Christmas."

"So now I'm Santa Clause."

"No, you're more like my daddy who gets me everything I want for Christmas. Is that cool with you?"

"If I'm your daddy, you know what that means?"

"I'm afraid to hear what you gotta say." Passion gazed at Deion affectionately, with the kind of eyes that girls had when they liked a guy. He bit down slowly on his bottom lip and at that moment, Passion wished she could kiss him. Not only was he looking fine as fuck, he was wearing cologne she recognized—Aventis by Creed. She didn't remember him having that on the first time they'd met.

"Me being your daddy won't be that bad."

"Tell me more."

"I might have to spank you if you get out of line."

"Oooh. That sounds fun."

"We'll make it fun."

"When are we going to New York?"

"In a few days. I got some business I need to handle and then we out."

"What kind of business?" she pried.

"We gettin' kinda nosey, ain't we?"

Passion threw her hands up playfully and said, "Hey, I'm just asking you a question." Deion gave her five one hundred-dollar bills, as if telling her to shut up, don't ask him shit and just take the money. "Thank you, Daddy"

"This ain't for you, this is for my son," he teased.

"Well Demonte says thank you."

"Oh, that's his name?"

"That's a damn shame, you don't even know your son's name," Passion joked.

"I need to meet him."

"So you plan on sticking around."

"I hope so."

"I hope so too."

"Really?"

"Yep. Quiet as kept, I'm so tired of the games these Atlanta Niggas be playing." This conversation was getting a little too serious for Deion so he decided to change the direction it was going.

"Hey, do you know a girl in the club named Paris?"

"Yeah, the girl that introduced me to you."

"That's her. I forgot about that."

"We're not besties or nothing like that but I know her. Why?"

"Give this to her," he said, handing her a wad of cash.

Passion counted the money. "Why are you giving this ho money?"

"She danced for me."

"So you getting dances on credit?"

"No. I accidently gave her the same counterfeit money I gave you." Passion folded the money and stuffed it in her bra. Deion stood from the booth, leaned over, and kissed Passion on the cheek. "Thanks, babe."

"So when you gonna give me my spanking?"

"Real soon. You can believe that. I'm gonna

give you a spanking you'll never forget." Deion exited the Waffle House, got into the Lamborghini and pulled away.

"Man, this Mexican has been texting the shit out of me," 2Glocks informed Deion as soon as he got back in the car.

"You told him we're on our way, right?"

"Of course I did, but the motherfucker is getting impatient."

"Fuck him! We got what he wants. He wants this money."

"He wants us to meet him at the warehouse."

"Warehouse? What you talkin' 'bout?"

"It's the warehouse off Old National. It's in the back of some office building, away from the road. Kinda in the cut."

"So you been there before?"

"To a couple, but I'm telling you dude, these guys have warehouses of this shit. They in this deep."

"Guide me to the spot."

"Hold up, he just hit me again," 2Glocks said.

"What did he say?"

"Come to the back of the warehouse and park between the blue pickup truck and the van."

"Cool."

Deion stopped to gas up the Lamborghini, so it

took them twenty minutes and not the ten minutes that 2Glocks had promised. They drove to the back of the warehouse and maneuvered between the blue pickup and a black van. Deion recognized the young Mexican who had been at Jose's house. This time he was wearing a blue headband and not the red one. His wife-beater exposed huge muscles and a tattoo of the Virgin of Guadalupe.

Muscles signaled for them to get out of the car. Deion was getting the money together. It was in a computer bag on the floor of the car between his legs.

"Hold on a second. Let me text Jose," 2Glocks said, while Deion was getting the money.

Muscles waved for them to get out of the car and he was looking impatient. "Give me a second," 2Glocks yelled out, after rolling down the window. 2Glocks texted Jose while Deion skimmed through the money one last time to make sure it was all there.

Muscles shouted something in Spanish, then flashed an AR-15. 2Glocks was the first to see what was going down and warned Deion. "Yo, get the fuck down!" 2Glocks warned. Sixteen shots entered into the passenger side of the Lamborghini door.

Deion grabbed his gun from his waist with his cell phone in his other hand. He opened the door, crawled out and dove underneath the car, his iPhone shattering. Between the commotion and gunfire he heard 2Glocks cry out, "I'm too young to die!"

More shots continued to ring in the air, as both men tried not to get caught in the crossfire. Deion saw Muscles' Air Jordans from underneath the car, but there was no way for him to get a good shot, plus he remembered there was a van on the other side of the car.

"I'm gonna die. Please, somebody help me," 2Glocks moaned. Deion wanted to help his friend but he had lost sight of Muscles. He heard somebody running but could no longer see the Air Jordans. He cocked his gun and crawled from underneath the car. Deion saw Muscles running but he was too far away to get a good shot at him.

2Glocks was sprawled in the seat, his mouth open, his white t-shirt soaked in blood. Deion grabbed his hand and placed his thumb on his wrist but there was no pulse. His friend was dead. Deion looked at the scattered money on the floor but there was no time to gather it. He needed to call somebody but his screen was cracked. He couldn't see his address book. He flipped his screen until he made it to his call log. Unable to see the contacts he pressed a random name and was relieved when he recognized Reggie's voice on the other end of the phone.

"I need you to come get me!"

"What's wrong?"

"Man, it's done went all bad. All motherfuckin' bad. 2Glocks is dead."

"What?"

"He just got murdered!"

"How did this happen? Where you at?"

"I'm at this warehouse on Old National."

"Gotta be more specific than that, homie."

"I don't know where the fuck I am. I can't think right now. Just come and get me."

"So how did 2Glocks get---"

"Quit asking me all these fuckin' questions," Deion roared, cutting Reggie off mid-sentence. "Just come and get me, man. I'll give you the details when you get here."

"I don't know where to go."

"Do you know where the Waffle House is?"

"Yes."

"I'ma try to make it there."

"Okay. I'll be there in half an hour."

"Cool." Deion sprinted to the front of the building. No sign of the Mexicans, or anybody for that matter. He jogged in the direction of the Waffle

House. Reggie was waiting in the parking lot in a Black Dodge Charger.

"Not a word to Alex, man," Deion said, as soon as he got in the car.

"I ain't' saying shit. What happened?"

"It's a long fuckin' story. Take me home, I just wanna get in bed."

"What about the car? What about 2Glocks?"

"Nigga, we can't go back over there tonight. This motherfucker was shooting something like an AR-15. I will worry about that shit in the morning."

There was so much Reggie wanted to ask Deion, but he didn't; instead they rode in silence.

Chapter 14
THIS CAN'T BE LIFE

Alex received a call from an anonymous phone number and at first he didn't answer. His phone rang again and this time he picked up. "Hello?"

"Hey, Alex."

"Who is this?"

"This J.D."

"I've been looking for you."

"Look man, I know what I did to you was wrong."

"You damn right it was wrong. I want my fuckin' money, J.D., and if you ain't talkin' 'bout my money, then get the fuck off my phone."

"Alex, I didn't want to do that to you man. Really I didn't, but I was in a lot of debt. I had to make the money up or else."

"J.D., you got my money or not? That's all I need to know."

"I'm working on it, man."

"Call me back when the work is done and you got my bread, and I mean all of it." Alex ended the call but his phone rang again. This time it was Joaquin.

"Hey."

"Alex, watch the news in fifteen minutes."

"For what?"

"Just watch the news. We will talk about it later." Alex hung up with Joaquin and grabbed the remote. When he turned to the news he was instantly transfixed. He realized all that death Joaquin had warned him about was in full motion.

Alex had once again started his day Instagram-stalking Tierney. He scrolled through the pics of her posing damn near every which way but nude. She seemed to be enjoying herself in each shot, but one with her lounging on the back of a red Porsche held Alex's attention, though he didn't know why. Right when he was about to log out he noticed the license plate on the Porsche—ArkTEK. What the fuck? He couldn't believe this shit. His ex was fucking the old-ass architect? His heart sank. Not because he wanted Tierney back, but because he knew that if it wasn't for him, she wouldn't have ever met the man. He tried calling her scandalous ass, but the number wasn't working. Right when Alex was about to try another number he had on her, he saw Joaquin was calling.

"The news is on," Joaquin informed him for the second day in a row. Alex knew that meant there was more blood shed.

"We have breaking news. An entire family was murdered in Southeast Atlanta," the news anchorwoman said. Alex sat and listened as the female correspondent described the house and a family that had been murdered in an upscale neighborhood. One of the neighbors said the family pretty much kept to themselves, the kids were nice, and the man of the house had described himself as a music executive. That same neighbor said that he had noticed a lot of expensive cars like Rolls Royces and Bentleys, but hadn't been alarmed by it because cars like that were a common sight.

Alex shook his head thinking about Joaquin having the whole family wiped out. Though he didn't know the murdered man he felt bad for the wife and the kids. He was about to power down his TV set when the anchor switched the story to another dead body being found in a yellow Lamborghini in the back of the Green Ridge warehouses and Business Park off Old National Highway. The man had apparently died of multiple gunshot wounds. Police were still investigating.

Alex recognized that Lamborghini because it was the rental car he had begged Deion to take back. He immediately called him but didn't get an answer. He kept dialing. The phone kept going to voicemail. He grabbed a t-shirt, pair of sweatpants and some sneakers and sprinted out the door. He had to find out if that was his partner.

When Alex arrived at Deion's crib, security called up but couldn't get an answer. Because they knew who Alex was, they let him up anyway. Alex had to bang on the door for a few before Deion finally answered.

"Man, you had my ass worried as fuck," Alex scoffed, walking past Deion.

"I was sleeping. The way you barging up in here, Reggie must've opened his big mouth and told you what happened," Deion frowned, closing the door.

"Nah, Reggie didn't tell me shit."

"Then what got you so scared?"

"I saw that damn bright-ass Lambo on the news wit' a body being pulled out. Nigga, I thought that might be you."

Deion sat down on the sofa and put his head down. He buried his face in his hands for a second before speaking. "It wasn't me, it was 2Glocks."

"Not 2Glocks. Who wanted that nigga dead?"

"Man, this is all J.D. fault."

"J.D.?"

"Yeah, that fake fuckin' money he gave us. I can't wait to kill that nigga."

"Just tell me what happened."

"Remember I told you that I gave some of that counterfeit money to the Mexican dude I bought that cocaine from?"

"Yeah, I remember that."

"When I mentioned it to 2Glocks he said Jose didn't say shit to him about it and figured that they was bringing in so much paper he hadn't noticed yet. Well, 2Glocks wanted to make another buy and when we got to the spot to meet them, they came out tryna kill motherfuckers. So clearly they already knew about the bootleg money and was pissed the fuck off."

"Damn! This shit done got ugly!"

"I know. And Alex, don't lecture me saying I

should've never fucked wit' those Mexicans on that coke shit. 'Cause at the end of the day, if J.D. hadn't fucked us over on that money then none of this shit would've went down."

"J.D. called me the other day too."

"And said what?" Deion questioned, rising up from the sofa, getting even more pissed that he wasn't able to get his hands on J.D. right then.

"He apologized saying he was wrong but he was in a lot of debt."

"Don't nobody wanna hear that grown-ass man's sad story. Fuck him!"

"That's basically what I said. I told him not to call me again until he got our money. But that still ain't gone bring 2Glocks back and make shit right wit' the Mexican dude you fuckin' wit'."

"I know. And I damn sure gotta get that situation corrected."

"Why don't you just tell him you don't do business like that but somebody fucked you over and you want to give him back the money you owe and be done wit' it."

"Man, you always make shit sound so easy. That nigga don't want to hear nothin' I got to say, and honestly at this point neither do I. I almost fuckin' died and 2Glocks is dead."

"I feel you. So what you gon' do?"

"You don't need to know."

"Yes I do, 'cause what you do affects me too. You don't think once the police trace that Lambo back to you, it's gon' put you on they radar?"

"I got that covered. None of that paperwork is in my name. The dude I rented it from already got his story together when the police come knockin'."

"I hope you right. The last thing you want to be caught up in is a murder investigation."

"I know this. That's why I'm tryna get some rest so I can get my mind right and figure this shit out."

"Cool. I'll let you go back to bed but I'm telling you, Deion, you have to be more careful." Deion nodded his head and showed Alex the door. Once he was gone he reached for his phone.

"Popcorn, I need your help wit' something. Meet me at that Starbucks in an hour." Since Alex had woken him up, Deion decided to start coming up with his exit plan now instead of later.

Chapter 15
LAND OF SNAKES

"Alex, what do you want? I told you not to show up here anymore," Tierney said with an attitude.

"I came over here to get closure."

"I thought we already did that."

"Maybe you did, but I didn't."

"Alex, I'm not trying to have some long, drawn out conversation with you, especially when I've said all I have to say."

"All I'm asking for is five minutes. I think you can at least give me that." Tierney moved over to the side, allowing Alex to come in.

"Five minutes, that's all you got because I'm expecting company."

"Let me guess. Milton the filthy rich, old-ass architect." The stank look on Tierney's face instantly disappeared and was replaced with one of guilt. "I guess that means I'm right."

"Who I'm seeing is none of your concern."

"Yeah, you right, not anymore, but it's fucked up that you met your new man while you were with me. My question is, was you fuckin' him too?"

"Of course not. I was only having sex with you during our relationship, just like you were only having sex with me," Tierney said sarcastically.

"I may not have been the ideal boyfriend that you wanted but I always took good care of you. For you to allow me to spend my money on you and pay your bills while you fuckin' another nigga is foul."

"Whatever, Alex."

"Whatever is right. I get it now. You're just an ungrateful trick. But that's cool. You go 'head and let that old man trick off on you, but the shit ain't gone last."

"Just because you didn't want to wife me, you think that the next man won't. Nigga, please. I got this. You need to worry about yourself. I've moved on to bigger and better things and I suggest you do the same, although I doubt it will ever happen for you. Ain't no woman going to be sitting around waiting for you to get your shit together and put a ring on it, so good luck to you. Now get the fuck out, Alex."

Alex stood in front of Tierney's door for a few minutes after she slammed it in his face. It took all his self-control not to put his fist through the wall. The initial hurt when she ended their relationship had now turned to anger. Alex had been so busy hustling in the streets, building up his money, he hadn't realized Tierney had been playing him, or at least that's how he felt. Alex decided at that moment he was done stressing over his ex. Shit happens and it was time for him to move on.

"I need you to find me a crew of niggas that all they do is kill," Deion informed Popcorn as they sat in Starbucks, having what he considered a business meeting. Starbucks was becoming Deion's personal office, and for the location, he was getting prime real estate for a cheap-ass price.

"I think I might know the perfect team. They like twelve or thirteen deep and all they like to do is kill."

"That's what I'm talkin' 'bout. Make sure they go hard, 'cause I want them to take down Jose and his men."

"Got you."

"But if they can handle the job, they'll be well-compensated. I just want that nigga dead. As long as we both walking the streets of Atlanta, I ain't gon' feel safe."

"So when you tryna make this happen?"

"As soon as we get this team of killers together. I already got somebody keeping tabs on Jose now. I'm making sure they watching his every step so when it's time to make our move we know what we're dealing wit'."

"The moment I leave here I'll get on it."

"Good. I'll also have that other stuff for you tomorrow. I need to start stackin' these millions."

"I'm wit' you, cowboy. After I speak to them boys I'll hit you up, but I'll definitely see you tomorrow," Popcorn said before leaving.

Deion sat in Starbucks thinking how lovely shit will be if Popcorn came through with those killers. Deion not only planned on taking Jose's life but he also planned on taking everything he left behind. Because of 2Glocks, Deion knew the locations of the warehouses Jose had that stored all of his coke. Once Jose was gotten rid of permanently, he was going to raid all those spots and keep it for himself. Deion knew if he got access to all of Jose's drugs it would give him all the power.

While Deion was leaving Starbucks, he continued having dreams of all the money and power he would soon have if he could get rid of Jose. Deion was so engrossed in these dreams that at first he didn't notice the two men standing near his pickup truck. It wasn't until he got midway to his ride that the sun seemed to flicker light on the chrome that one of the men was clutching, Deion realized what was up. He recognized the goons from when they were outside Popcorn's apartment waiting for him. The difference was, last time Deion was at least strapped, but today he had left his crib so quickly, he had nothing.

Fuck! How the hell am I gonna get away from these niggas? I ain't got no heat or nothin'. Fuck it! It's now or never, Deion said to himself. With limited options he made the decision to take his chances and haul ass. He did a quick U-turn and bolted in the direction of a busy street. He figured the goons wouldn't want to open fire in broad daylight in front of numerous eyewitnesses, but they didn't give a fuck. Deion could hear gunshots flying in his direction, but he continued moving forward, accelerating his speed and never looking back. He hadn't ran this fast since he was a young kid growing up in the TechWood homes, doing petty crimes with Alex.

Between gunshots, Deion heard a car start up. So now one goon was chasing him on foot, blasting off, and another was behind the wheel of the car, ready to run him down. Deion was running so fast he could hear his rapid chest compressions. As he darted across the busy street, all he heard were cars blowing their horns and sudden stops as many vehicles were pressing down on their brakes to avoid hitting him. Deion finally came upon a strip mall and ran inside one of the stores, sweating profusely. He found the bathroom, locked the door and turned on the faucet. Deion drenched his face in water before looking up to catch his reflection in the mirror.

"Damn, when it rains it pours," Deion said, shaking his head.

Chapter 16
LIFE IS WHAT YOU MAKE IT

"Alex, I was surprised to hear from you so soon, although I've missed you," Isabella said, kissing him when he entered her hotel room.

"I missed you too, but my call was more about business."

"I thought business was going well. Joaquin said you were pleased with the new product."

"He's right, but I need more. You said your family has direct connections. I can keep getting work from Joaquin but you can also supply me."

"All this is true, but where did this sudden change come from? A couple months ago you wanted no part of moving heroin. I have to convince you that this would be the right business decision for you. Now you want to move even more product?"

"I need to get my money up, that's all."

"I think it's more than that. Alex, I like you. You can talk to me about anything."

"I'm not sure if I can talk to you about this."

"Why, does it have to do with another woman?" Isabella could tell by the look on Alex's face and his unwillingness to answer her question that it did. "Alex, I'm not going to deny that I love having sex with you, but I am a married woman and I don't expect for you to be committed to me."

"Her name is Tierney. She's my ex. I found out she's now with some rich older man who's an architect that she met while with me. It's like she's trying to shit in my face." Alex felt a sense of relief being able to express his feelings to Isabella. This was exactly what he needed.

"Your ego is bruised."

"Yeah, that's fair to say."

"I understand. A man's pride and ego is normally the biggest motivating factor in all that he does."

"It's more than that. I want Tierney to know that I have just as much as the new man she's with."

"Then what...are you hoping she'll take you back?"

"Hell no! I don't want her scandalous ass back.

I've always known Tierney wasn't the woman for me, but I don't appreciate how she ended things. I always treated her good and never disrespected her. All I asked is that she did the same. But no, she had me taking care of her while she was fuckin' the next nigga behind my back. I feel like she played me and I don't like that feeling."

"No one does," Isabella stated. Alex could tell that Isabella was talking about herself and the situation with Joaquin. After the Tierney situation, Alex completely understood where Isabella was coming from. "So what are you trying to accomplish now? Is your ultimate goal still to make enough money to leave the game behind?"

"Nope, I now want all the power. I not only want to dominate Atlanta but any other place I can get my hands on too."

"Say no more. I told you I wanted to help you be the King and that's exactly what I'm going to do. I promise you."

"You are so fuckin' sexy, especially when you discussing business," Alex said, slipping off Isabella's satin lace halter slip. He kissed her neck and then went directly to her full breasts, putting his mouth on her erect nipples.

"Ahhhh," Isabella purred softly. Alex lifted her

up and laid her down on the bed. Looking at every voluptuous curve on Isabella's body made Alex's dick so hard. When he entered inside her warm, welcoming pussy it seemed that all his stress melted away. For the next hour he got lost in her wetness and stopped obsessing over his yearning for wealth and power.

"Damn, baby, where you been? I haven't heard from you in weeks. I thought you forgot about me."

"How could I forget about you? I just been dealing wit' a lot of shit."

"Is everything cool now?"

"Somewhat. I got things under control."

"Does that mean you ready to take our trip to New York?"

"That's why I'm calling you." Deion could hear Passion sighing over the phone as if she already knew what he was about to say. "We can't make the trip right now. I know you disappointed but I'll make it up to you."

"That's like your favorite line, but you never make it up to me."

"How 'bout you meet me over at Phipps Plaza

in an hour."

"I'm not trying to window shop."

"Neither am I."

"Then I guess I'll see you in an hour."

Deion smiled when he hung up with Passion. He was actually looking forward to seeing her. The last few weeks had Deion feeling like he was lucky just to wake up and see another day. After almost being killed twice within a matter of days, Deion had been keeping a very low profile. Meeting Passion at Phipps was his first real outing in weeks. He had decided not to make any major moves until he got rid of Jose, and he also added Travis to that list.

As Deion was grabbing his car keys to walk out the door, he saw that Popcorn was calling him. "What up, man?"

"I got some news for you. Can we link up to discuss?"

"Yeah, meet me over at Phipps in twenty."

"Cool...see you in a minute."

Popcorn was standing directly in front of the Gucci store when Deion arrived. Deion was tempted to get Passion a purse that he noticed in the front store window as a surprise, but decided against it. He thought she would have more fun picking out her own goodies.

"Man, I can't believe you finally decided to show your face in the daytime," Popcorn joked. He was well aware that after the two different threats on Deion's life he had had basically gone MIA.

"Yeah, I'm meeting this chick up here. I thought it was time for me to get the fuck out my crib and live a little again. Constantly watching yo' back gets old after while. Come on, let's walk. So what you got for me?"

"Soon you won't have to worry about watching yo' back no more., unless you piss some mo' niggas off. Knowing yo' crazy ass, that might just happen."

"What can I say...I was born with a few screws loose. But I got that chicken so all that shit is overlooked."

"Nigga, you crazy. But foreal, them killa boys ready to move. They know which warehouse and the best time to catch Jose and his team."

"Yeah, make sure they put an extra bullet in that Muscle nigga for me too. Big goofy lookin' ass."

"I'll make sure to let them know."

"I'm serious."

"I know you are. Anything else?"

"Yeah, I'ma have a couple of other dudes that work for me cleaning out them warehouses as soon as I get word that Jose and his crew done. So I need those frequent updates. As a matter of fact, I'll have one of my workers tailing them niggas but I'll make sure he know to stay in the background. I don't want no fuckups."

"Trust me, for the amount of money you paying, there won't be any."

"Good. I would hate to have to hire another team to come in and kill these niggas 'cause they couldn't get the job done."

"We go way back. I wouldn't have put you on to these dudes if I wasn't positive they could deliver."

"That's what I need to hear," Deion nodded. "Let me go. The chick I'm meetin' just texted me letting me know she's here."

"You got her up in Phipps. Her head game must be ridiculous."

"I ain't even fucked this chick yet."

"What!"

"Nope. I'm expecting the head and pussy game to be on point though. If not, she'll just be another pretty bitch that got a few coins outta me. Like they say, it ain't trickin' if you got it."

"Deion, you that nigga," Popcorn said, giving

him the pound.

"So when is the hit going down?"

"Tomorrow around six thirty."

"Cool, I'll have my workers on alert. Talk to you soon.

As Popcorn was walking off, Passion was walking up. "There's my Daddy," Passion said with a wide grin on her face.

Deion hadn't seen Passion in awhile but she was still just as pretty as ever to him, even dressed down. She was wearing some low-cut jeans with a white razorback t-shirt and some wedge sneakers. She had on a full face of makeup with lashes and all, but because the colors were natural tones, her look was just right.

"You what I need today," Deion said, giving Passion a hug. She hugged him back even tighter as if she didn't want to let go. "You ready to shut this mall down?"

Passion leaned her body away from Deion and stared up at him with dollar signs in her eyes. She was smiling so hard, Deion thought her face might crack. "I sure am."

Deion spent the next couple of hours making Passion feel like Julia Roberts in Pretty Woman. She had bags from Valentino, Saks, Jimmy Choo,

Intermix, Gucci, Versace and just about every other high-end store besides Tiffany & Co. Deion didn't believe in buying women jewelry. He had bought clothes, shoes, cars, tits and even veneers but never a piece of jewelry. Deion always thought that was too personal and would give a woman the impression that she was special to him, so he stayed away from those type of gifts. It didn't matter though, because most women, including Passion, were thrilled to get whatever Deion was buying.

No man had ever splurged on Passion the way Deion had and she planned on showing him just how grateful she was. When they got back to his crib, Deion didn't have to say a word. Passion was naked and had his dick in her mouth before he could even offer her something to drink. But like Deion expected, her suck and fuck game were on point, which pleased him. Deion was now able to add Passion to his short list of keepers.

Chapter 17
THIS MY WORLD

In the last six months several things had changed for Alex. He was now moving more heroin than anybody else in Atlanta. He had also expanded his operation to several other cities, including a couple on the East Coast. The power he had craved was now his, and he had nobody but Isabella to thank for it. She kept her word and made sure that Alex stayed stocked with the purest and most potent heroin. There was only one other distributor that could somewhat compete with the product Alex had and that was the Get Money Crew.

Alex heard they were dealing with a connect out in Texas, but no matter how good their shit was, because of Alex's direct dealings with Isabella he was getting the best prices across the board. He was winning on both ends. He was also continuing to make his real estate investments with Danny, so he was also generating more legitimate money.

"Life is good right now," Alex said, as he sat across from Deion while dining at Bacchanalia.

"There used to be a time when we would've never felt comfortable in an upscale restaurant like this, but now it feels like we've always belonged," Deion said, scanning the menu.

"Hi, I'm Dahlia. I'll be your waitress for the evening. What can I get you all to drink?" Both Alex and Deion looked up at the same time to place a face with such a sweet, engaging voice.

"Damn, you are beautiful. Much too beautiful to be waitin' tables," Deion said to the woman. At first she seemed stunned by what he'd said, but she played it cool.

"Thank you, but I'm in school and the tips here help out a lot."

"Give me your number and within a week you'll never have to wait another table again."

"Why don't I give you both a moment to look over your menu and decide what you like. I'll be back shortly. Thanks."

"You scared that poor girl off. Why you do that?"

"Man, that bitch bad. I need her out of those black slacks and naked in my bed. Maybe I can have her do a threesome with Passion and me. She in school and clearly she need money. I'll have her pockets extra right."

"Everybody ain't for sale, Deion."

"Lies, nigga. Hold up...I gotta take this call. I'll be right back."

All Alex could do was shake his head at Deion. That was his best friend and he had nothing but love for him, but at the same time Deion's views on a lot of shit was fucked up to him. They were alike but different in so many ways.

"Hi, are you ready to order, or would you like to wait for you friend and I can come back?"

"No, you don't have to leave. You can go ahead and put my order in. My friend had to take a phone call so I'm not sure how long he'll be."

"Sure, what can I get you?" Alex was speechless for a second. He understood what Deion was talking about because the woman was absolutely breathtaking. She had a regal beauty to her.

"I apologize for staring at you. This isn't a line, but has anyone ever told you that you resemble Tika Sumpter?"

"Actually, they have," she smiled. Her teeth

were perfectly straight and white. When she smiled her entire face lit up.

"If you don't mind me asking, what are you in school for?"

"Child Psychology."

"Impressive."

"Thank you."

"I want to apologize for some of the things my friend said earlier."

"You don't have to. Trust me, I hear all sorts of things from men that come through here. Your friend was a little blunt, but I've heard worse," she laughed.

"It's good you have a sense of humor about it."

"I have no choice. I need the job."

"Would you mind if I asked for your number?"

"I would mind if you didn't." Alex noticed her eyes seemed to sparkle when she smiled and his strong attraction for her made him a tad uneasy.

"Put your number in my phone," he said, handing her his Samsung Galaxy. "Dahlia, I'm hoping you'll let me take you out."

"Well, that is the reason I'm giving you my number, isn't it?" she grinned.

"True that."

"I'll be right back. I just remembered I have to

bring out some food for another table."

"Take your time, I'm not going anywhere."

"Thanks," she said, handing Alex his phone before rushing off.

"Wait, hold up. Did I just see my bitch give you her number?" Deion questioned when he walked back up to the table.

"First off, her name is Dahlia and she's not yo' bitch. Secondly, yes I did ask for her number and I'ma take her out on a date."

"So the chick I was checkin' for, you takin' out on a date."

"You mean a chick we were both checkin' for, and she chose me."

"Whatever, you can have her. I already got too many broads in rotation."

"I'm sure you do. But before I forget, I meant to tell you that J.D. reached out to me again."

"That fat fuck been ghost all these months and he finally decided to reappear?"

"Yep, and he claims he has our money."

"After all this time, we should charge the motherfucker interest. So when is he bringing it?"

"He supposed to call me tomorrow. Said he'll be in town and wants to drop off the money to us."

"I'll believe that shit when I see it."

"I don't think he bullshitting. What was the point of calling after all this time if he didn't have our bread?"

"True. He probably lost all his connects and need to get some product from us. I ain't giving that nigga shit and you shouldn't either. It's because of him 2Glocks is dead and his kids gon' grow up without a father. So fuck J.D."

"I feel you on that."

"As a matter of fact, when I get my portion of the money back from that stank-breath fuck, I'm giving it to 2Glocks' mom to help take care of his kids."

"That's a good look, Deion. I know that would've meant a lot to 2Glocks. His family will appreciate that."

"I think I owe him that. Enough of this depressing talk...where our waitress at so we can order this food and eat?" Deion said, ready to change the topic.

Deion had a lot of fucked up ways, but it was moments like this that made Alex respect his childhood best friend and partner. He cared about the kids, and even with all the foul shit he did, there was still good in him.

Chapter 18
SPARKS WILL FLY

"I appreciate ya' coming through. I know you feelin' some type of way 'bout me and I deserve all of it," J.D. said, his arms crossing each other to represent his use of the term 'all'.

Both Alex and Deion stood in the middle of J.D.'s hotel room not saying a word. They just listened as he gave them some elaborate excuse as to why he had given them counterfeit money and the reason it took him so long to pay them back. After ten more minutes of listening to the bullshit, Deion couldn't take anymore.

"Man, we get it. You got yourself in a fucked up situation and instead of handling it like a man you decided to fuck us over instead. Now give us our cash so we can bounce."

"Deion, man, it ain't like that. I got nothin' but love for you and Alex. You gotta believe me."

"J.D., you have to understand that what you did caused a lot of unnecessary problems for us. It ain't easy to just say all is forgiven."

"I get that, Alex. But hopefully giving you all the money back," he said, handing over the duffel bag full of cash, "will make things better between us. 'Cause you know, I would like to continue doing business wit' you."

While J.D. started pleading his case, Deion took the bag from Alex and pulled out his pen to check if the bills were good.

"That money is real, I promise you, Deion."

"It better be. We don't have time to stand here and check every bill, but if we find out even one ain't good, we comin' to see you. But this time, won't be no talkin'."

"It's all there and it's all good, man. Once you see I'm being straight up, will ya' consider selling to me again?"

"Definitely," Deion answered. Alex glanced over at Deion but didn't say anything.

"That's what I'm talkin' 'bout," J.D. cheesed up, happy to hear he was back in the game.

"So how long you gon' be in town?" Deion

asked as they were walking out.

"Tomorrow I hit the road."

"Cool, have a safe trip back and we'll be in touch."

"A'ight. If you change yo' mind and decide you ready to start doing business again, I got some more money here," J.D. said, pointing over to another duffel bag, "to buy drugs."

"We'll think it over," Deion said, giving J.D. a pound before leaving.

"Man, what was that about? Last night you was adamant you didn't want to fuck wit' J.D. again. Now you telling him if his money is good then definitely," Alex said as they were getting on the elevator.

"I was fuckin' wit' him. I wanted to see if he was serious about all the money being good. You know I don't trust nothin' that come out his mouth."

"Yeah, but I think he tellin' the truth this time."

"Me too. Only 'cause he desperate to get back on."

"Yeah, and you left that nigga feeling hopeful too," Alex laughed.

"Damn sure did. Oh fuck!" Deion belted, patting his pockets.

"What is it?" Alex questioned, as they got off the elevator.

"I must've forgot my phone in J.D.'s room. I'll be right back."

"I'll wait for you down here in the lobby."

"That's okay, I got my car. You go 'head."

"Cool. If I don't talk to you tonight we'll get up tomorrow."

Deion got on the elevator and headed back up to J.D.'s room. Deion knocked on the door and he could tell J.D. was looking through the peephole.

"What up, you back already?" J.D. smiled. "I guess that means we're back in business."

"I guess it does. Let's talk numbers."

"Let's do it," J.D. said, closing the door. "Room service just brought up my food. You don't mind if I eat while we talk?"

"Nah, do yo' thing." While J.D. busied himself preparing to devour his meal, Deion reached behind his back, pulling out the .357 automatic with an extended clip and a silencer screwed onto it.

"This steak good as hell," J.D. smacked, oblivious to what was coming next.

"Enjoy your last meal, you fat fuck. This for 2Glocks," Deion spit, before releasing a bullet directly between J.D.'s eyes, blowing his brains out. What was left of his head fell flat down, resting on his steak. Deion looked around for the other duffel bag J.D had. He spotted it in the corner. Once Deion unzipped it and saw all the money, he grabbed it. "Now we even," he said, before making his exit.

"When you called asking to meet for drinks, I was pleasantly surprised," Dahlia smiled.

"Why were you surprised?"

"Because we just met last night. I figured you would probably try to play that 'I'm not pressed' role and wait at least a few days before you called. I'm glad I was wrong."

"Me too. I would hate to be so predictable."

"Being predictable can be good sometimes."

"Like when?"

"When you're in a committed relationship with someone and you like knowing their schedule is pretty consistent. It might be a little predictable, but it can also make the other person feel more secure in the relationship."

"That's an interesting point and very valid. I never thought about that before, but it's true."

"So why is a handsome, charming man like yourself single? You are single, right? I didn't see a ring, but that doesn't mean anything."

"I'm very single and I've never been married. The reason being is because I've been so focused on making money, that a relationship has always taken a backseat."

"That's unfortunate. It doesn't matter how successful you are and how much money you make if you don't have a family to share it with."

"You're right. My ex thought I was obsessed with making money and I was...I still am."

"How long ago did you and your ex break up?"

"It's been months. Why do you ask?"

"I want to make sure I'm not stepping into rebound territory. If you're not over your ex then I need to proceed with caution."

"No need to do that. I'm completely over her."

"Did things end badly?"

"Somewhat, but I learned a lot. I won't be making the same mistakes in my next relationship."

"That's very important."

"What about you? A beautiful woman like yourself, I know you must be fighting off the men."

"I've had a couple long-term relationships but I'm not with either one of them so clearly they weren't the men for me."

"What type of man are you looking for?"

"Honestly, I'm not looking. Between work and

school I barely have time to put any energy towards a relationship. That was the problem with my ex. He was going to school to be a doctor and between our schedules we could never find time to make it work. But they say, things that you really care about, you find the time. So maybe we just didn't care enough."

"Don't think I'm some crazy man when I say this to you."

"Say what?"

"I hope that you go out your way to make time for me, because there is just something about you I adore. I want you in my life."

"Wow, I wasn't expecting you to say that, but I'm glad you did." Dahlia leaned over and gently kissed Alex. It was so quick that Alex had to move in for another one. This time it was long and lingering.

"Where have you been all my life?" Alex whispered.

"Getting myself prepared so I would be ready to be with you."

Alex and Dahlia stared into each other's eyes. Alex couldn't understand why he felt so drawn to this woman. Yes, she was beautiful and smart, but it was more than that. From the moment he laid eyes on her he felt a connection. Something he never felt towards another woman. It actually scared him, but he decided not to let that fear keep him away. Instead, Alex was determined to dive right in.

"I want to know everything about you," Alex said.

"Okay, where do you want me to start?"

"At the beginning."

They spent the next several hours sitting at their table, talking all night. The only reason they stopped was because the lounge was closing. Instead of going home, they continued their conversation parked outside the lounge in Alex's car. Neither of them believed in love at first sight, but both felt that if it wasn't love then it was the closest thing to it.

Chapter 19
Forbidden Fruit

"Man, you a hard person to catch up with these days," Reggie said. "I've been trying to get over here to see you for weeks. Where you been?"

"You wouldn't believe me if I told you."

"Try me."

"I met somebody about a month ago and every chance I get, I try to spend it with her. I guess you can say I got it bad."

"Is this some sort of joke?" Reggie asked, putting down the remote control and leaning back in the chair.

"Nope. This is the real deal. This is that thing I've wanted to feel for a woman but never did. Now I have, and it's incredible."

"Nigga, shut up. I ain't here for yo' jokes."

"Reggie, look at me. I'm not joking. Her name is Dahlia and I'm crazy about her."

"Okay, say this isn't a joke and all this is true. You just said you've only known her for a month. How you gon' be all crazy for a chick you've only known for a month unless that pussy got you sprung?"

"That's not it, we haven't even had sex yet."

"You haven't had sex with this woman and you talkin' like this?"

"Trust me, for the first couple weeks I was saying that same shit. But I guess I'm one of the lucky ones."

"What you mean?"

"I've heard people talk about meeting their soul mates. Or meeting someone for the first time and knowing that's the person you're supposed to spend the rest of your life with. I never believed none of that bullshit until now. She's the one."

"She the one for what?"

"I think she's the one I'm supposed to spend the rest of my life with."

"Hold up," Reggie said, rising from the chair. "Slow down. You moving way too fast on this. You have to at least hit it first, before you even think about saying she the one."

"Says you, not me. I know everything I need

to. This weekend I'm actually taking her to go meet my mother."

"You done lost yo' mind. You ain't neva taken a chick to meet your mother."

"That's because Dahlia ain't any chick. I've been wanting to settle down for a long time, but I wasn't rushing it because I hadn't met the right woman, until now. When you know something is right, it doesn't take long to see it."

"You really are serious."

"That's what I've been saying. You just figuring that out?"

"Then congratulations, man. I'm happy for you. Since I first met you, you've always been on your paper chase. So you the last person I ever thought would meet someone you'd want to settle down with."

"I thought the same thing, and I was okay with that. But now that I've found that special woman, I don't know how I went so long without her."

"Foreal though, I'm happy for you, but enough of this mushy stuff. I gotta get used to even having these types of conversations wit' you."

"Well you better start getting used to it."

"Yeah, yeah, yeah."

"So what else been going on?"

"Same shit. Between you runnin' all that heroin and Deion moving all that coke, the two of you keep a nigga busy."

"Yeah, I still can't believe how Deion just strong-armed himself into taking over Jose's operation. That nigga got balls, but he always did, even as kids."

"Well, ain't much a dead man can do. Speaking of dead men, did you hear about J.D.?"

"What about J.D.?"

"He got killed."

"We just saw him about a month ago when he gave us back our money. He probably had fucked somebody else over wit' that counterfeit bullshit, but unlike us, they wasn't so forgiving. Do you know what happened?"

"It happened at whatever hotel he was staying at. Somebody came in there and shot him."

"J.D. had some fucked up ways, and what he did was foul, but I liked dude. I hate he had to go out like that."

"Yeah, but like you said. When you do foul shit to motherfuckers, eventually it will catch up to you."

"True, indeed."

"What up, Demonte?"

"Hey, Uncle Deion. I'm on my way outside to play with my friends."

"Have a good time. Here, take some money," Deion said, reaching in his pocket and pulling out a few twenty dollar bills, "in case you and your friends get hungry," he continued, putting the money in Demonte's hand.

"Thank you so much, Uncle Deion. I'll see you later on." Demonte gave Deion a hug before running outside to play.

"Hey baby," Passion said, coming downstairs right when Deion was closing the door. "I see why Demonte love him some Deion. You spoil him about as much as you spoil me."

"Yeah, but yo' spoiling cost a lot mo' money."

"You don't think I'm worth it?"

"Of course I do. Didn't I get you off that pole?"

"You sure did. Now let me take you upstairs and show you how grateful I am."

Deion watched Passion's ass sway from side to side as she led him upstairs to her bedroom. Due to her masterful skills of fucking and sucking, Deion not only put Passion in constant rotation amongst his chicks, he moved her up to the top as his favorite. Once that happened he had to pull her out the strip club because he wanted her to be on call to please him whenever and however. In exchange, Deion paid all Passion's bills, gave her a monthly allowance for shopping and other leisure activities, bought her a BMW and even paid for Demonte's private school.

Although Passion could fuck, was sexy and catered to his every desire, what he liked most about her was her relationship with her son. Since she no longer had to strip to take care of Demonte, Passion gladly took on the role as a soccer mom. But when she entered that bedroom, she became Deion's personal whore, just the way he liked it.

Deion was in his Bentley Coupe listening to Drake when he noticed his gas light come on. Passion had worn him out so he didn't feel like stopping. But it was either pull into Exxon or take the chance of running out of gas and having to push his ride. Deion opted to stop at Exxon. When he pulled into the gas station, his eyes immediately became fixated on a pretty chocolate brown beauty who was pumping gas.

Deion pulled up right next to the woman and

rolled his window down. "You need help with that?"

The woman didn't even turn around to acknowledge Deion. Instead she kept pumping her gas, ignoring his question. That infuriated Deion and only made him try harder to get her attention. He pulled his car over to one of the pumps and walked over to his target, determined to get her number.

"You didn't hear me talkin' to you?" he asked in a cocky tone.

"Excuse me," the woman said with an attitude, finally turning around to see the man who was now working her very last nerve.

"Ain't this some shit. You that waitress chick."

"Yeah, and the name is Dahlia."

"Dahlia...I like that name."

"Thanks. Now can you excuse me? I need to finish pumping my gas."

"You still not trying to give me those digits."

"You do know I'm dating Alex...your friend."

"Ya' still dating? I didn't think it was that serious."

"Why would you think that?"

"Look at what you driving." Deion nodded his head towards Dahlia's modest older-model car. "My man can't be serious about you if he got you riding around in this. See, if you was my girl, you'd have the best of everything."

"Listen, things are very serious between Alex and me, but even if we weren't I wouldn't date you. You're not my type."

"I'm every woman's type."

"Then you won't have any problem leaving me alone and going to bother some other woman."

"You one of those high post broads...but I like that. We'll see each other again. And after Alex dumps you, I'll still be willing to give you a try," Deion winked, before walking back to his car.

Chapter 20
LOVE IN THE SKY

"You wanna play again? I never get tired of kickin' yo' ass," Deion mocked Popcorn after beating him for the third time playing pool at The Independent in Midtown.

"Ain't nothin', cowboy. I got you this game."

"Whatever. You been sayin' that shit the last three games," Deion said, hitting the solid color ball in the third pocket. Right when he was about to shoot again, he noticed some dude coming towards their table. Deion put his cue stick down and nodded his head at Popcorn. On the low, Popcorn turned his head to see what had grabbed Deion's attention.

"Oh, what up? This my nigga Tommy I was tellin' you about," Popcorn said, speaking to the dude. "Tommy, this Deion."

"Good to meet you."

"Popcorn said you tryna put in some work," Deion said, skipping the formalities. The Independent was Deion's other office. He liked having certain business meetings here because it was loud and smoke-filled, which meant motherfuckers weren't paying attention to what you were saying, and if they were, they couldn't hear shit.

"Yeah, something like that."

"You down wit' GMC, why you need work from me?"

"Them my brothers but I want to branch out on my own. GMC is deep and only a few niggas in the crew is makin' that bread. The rest of us are basically low-level workers."

"I get that. My man Popcorn has vouched for you and I know he only fuck wit' motherfuckers about they business."

"True, and all I want to do is make some real money. I got kids to support."

"Popcorn got your information. I'll be in touch wit' you soon."

"Appreciate that, man," Tommy said before saying bye to both men.

"What you think?" Popcorn asked once Tommy was gone.

"I think I can use him. Young nigga and hungry. I'm positive the top dogs at GMC workin' the fuck out them boys so he definitely know these streets. Because they ain't feedin' that boy right is gon' be our gain."

"Yep. You right about that. Between all the coke and heroin you and Alex moving, the two of you are GMC's biggest competitors. They don't need none of they crew members coming over to our side."

"It's too late now, 'cause I'm definitely putting that lil' nigga to work," Deion stated, before going back to kicking Popcorn's ass in pool.

"When you said you wanted me to take a ride with you, I didn't know you meant the airport," Dahlia said, while sitting in First Class next to Alex.

"When you told me you had a couple days off from work and no classes, I thought it would be nice to get away. It's only Miami, but a change of scenery is always nice."

"What do you mean only Miami? I've never been there. I'm looking forward to it. Great weather, beaches and most importantly, you."

"That's how I feel too."

"Does taking me on this trip mean we're serious?" Dahlia questioned in a cynical way before laughing.

"Huh?" Alex gave her a perplexed look, confused by her question.

"It was somewhat of a joke. I ran into your friend Deion the other day."

"Where?"

"At the gas station."

"What did he say?"

"He was trying to hit on me and I reminded him I was dating you. He made the comment that he didn't think we were that serious because of the car I was driving."

"That sound like some silly shit Deion would say, but he's harmless."

"Are we serious?"

"Of course. You know how I feel about you," Alex said, taking Dahlia's hand.

"Then why did Deion feel he could try and talk to me?"

"Deion is my best friend and business partner but I don't really discuss my personal relationships with him. He hasn't seen me with you and I haven't mentioned you to him since we met at the restaurant, so he probably assumed nothing ever came of it."

"I see," Dahlia said, turning towards the window and looking outside at the clouds.

"Baby, just because I haven't talked to Deion about you don't mean shit. You met my mother and I have never brought a woman to meet my mother. And I did tell my friend Reggie about you. I told him you were the one. I love you, Dahlia," Alex said out loud to her for the first time.

"Really?" Dahlia turned back toward Alex and he could see the sparkle in her eyes that had left for a second had now returned.

"Yes, and if I have to buy you a new car or house to prove that to you or any other non-believer, I will."

"You don't have to do that. I don't need material things for you to show me that you love me. All I need is this right here, us being together, because I love you too."

Alex felt truly blessed to have Dahlia in his life. She represented the goodness that countered all the bad in his life. He'd felt it before, but this very moment confirmed to him that he was ready.

When they arrived at the W South Beach, Dahlia

instantly fell in love with the over 1,300 square foot bungalow they were staying in. There was a beautiful shell chandelier hanging from the nine-foot soaring ceilings with amazing artwork on each wall. After looking around the three floors, Dahlia stepped through the expansive private glass balcony that showcased breathtaking views of the beach and ocean.

"This place is beyond beautiful. Thank you for bringing me here. No one has ever done anything this nice for me before."

"I want to do so much more. Let's go for a walk on the beach."

"Sure." Alex took Dahlia's hand and they headed toward the beach as the sun began to set.

"Could you get used to this?"

"What do you mean?"

"Allowing me to spoil you?"

"Alex, I don't want you to feel like you have to spoil me in order to make me happy. Of course, luxury living is like having a dream life. But if it was just the two of us living in a one bedroom apartment, I would be just as happy."

"I know you would, but I want to spoil you. It's my way of showing you how much I appreciate you coming into my life and making me so happy."

"You make me happy too. This is like heaven on earth. And this warm sand feels so good on my feet. I wish I had a week off of work instead of only a couple days so we could stay longer."

"No worries. When we go on our honeymoon maybe we'll travel the world for sixty days."

"What did you say?"

"I said, Dahlia Duncan, will you marry me?" Alex was on bended knee.

The beach was quiet except for the soft crash of waves against the shore and the faint call of seagulls. The wind was blowing lightly and what was left of the shimmering sunlight had the sand sparkling like thousand tiny jewels. Alex was holding an eleven-carat radiant cut diamond.

"I don't know what to say," Dahlia said, as her eyes swelled up with tears.

"Say yes, unless you don't want to marry me."

"Of course I want to marry you. I just can't believe you're ready to marry me."

"I do, with all my heart I want you to be my wife. So I'll ask you again. Dahlia Duncan, will you marry me?"

"Yes! Yes! Yes! I will marry you." Alex slipped the ring on Dahlia's finger and he felt like it was the happiest day of his life.

That night Alex and Dahlia made love for the very first time. He took his time exploring every inch of her body. The softness of her skin felt like the finest silk. When Alex entered inside her warmth, with each stroke not only was he looking forward to Dahlia being his wife but he also hoped they were creating a child together.

Chapter 21
LUST, ENVY...GREED

"Alex, I'm so happy to see you. I know business is booming but I haven't seen you in weeks. The last time I did it was only briefly to give you your new shipment. I hope you finally have time for me today," Isabella said, as she sat down on the couch in the sitting room of her hotel suite.

"Actually I don't. I came over to talk to you about something."

"This sounds serious." Isabella reached for her glass of champagne on the table and took a sip.

"You know these last few months I've made millions and millions of dollars because of you."

"I told you, you would."

"And you were right, and I thank you."

"From your tone it sounds like you're about to

end things between us."

"I am. I'm about to head in a new direction in my life. I'm ready to finally give up the game."

"I'm surprised. I thought you were enjoying your newfound power."

"I was, but I found something, or shall I say someone, that I enjoy more."

"You met someone?" Alex could hear the pain in Isabella's voice, but he knew she deserved to hear the truth from him.

"Yes. Her name is Dahlia. We're engaged to be married."

"When did this happen?"

"About a month ago."

"Alex, don't you think it's too soon to be making this decision? You've only been engaged to this woman for a month. You need to give yourself more time."

"This is what I want. I don't need more time."

"Fine, so you no longer want to do business, but that doesn't have to change our personal relationship."

"Isabella, I'm getting married. I have no intentions on cheating on my fiancée or my wife. So our relationship is over."

Isabella quickly gulped down the rest of her

champagne before standing up. She walked over to the huge window overlooking the city. Alex didn't know if he should go over there or let her be.

"You really are a good man, Alex. If only my husband took his vows seriously, maybe I could have a real marriage."

"You are an incredible woman, Isabella. If Joaquin doesn't appreciate you maybe it's time for you to move on. You deserve to be with a man who will love and value you."

"If only it was that easy. Enough about my pathetic marriage; this is about you. I'm going to miss you and what we shared, but I'm sincerely happy for you. Your fiancé must be an amazing woman. I hope she knows what an incredible man she's marrying." Isabella walked over to Alex and gave him a goodbye kiss. "If you ever need me, I'll be there."

Alex left Isabella's hotel suite, hoping that she would be able to find the same happiness that he had. She had always been good to him and Alex wanted nothing but the best for her.

Deion and Passion arrived at Bone's Restaurant at the exact same time as Reggie and his date. They were there to meet Alex but had no idea what it was about.

"We're here to meet Alex Miller," Deion said to the hostess.

"Yes, he hasn't arrived yet but I can go ahead and seat you all in he Private Dining, Room G. Follow me, please."

"Do you have any idea what this dinner is about?" Deion asked Reggie as they headed towards the private room.

"Nope. He just told me to come and bring a date."

"That's the same shit he told me. He needs to get here soon, 'cause I'm starvin.'"

"Me too."

Deion and Reggie sat down and continued making small talk and the women did the same. While they waited, Deion ordered a bottle of champagne and appetizers.

"Let me call Alex and see what's taking him so long," Reggie said, reaching for his phone. Before he had a chance to dial it Alex walked in with Dahlia.

"Yo, that's Alex woman. Damn she bad," Reggie said to Deion. He glanced over at his date, making sure she hadn't heard him.

Deion had seen Dahlia a couple times and

he always thought she was a beautiful woman, but tonight she was simply stunning. Alex had definitely upgraded her. Dahlia had on a butterscotch belted dress with crossover detailing at the chest. She finished the look with a nude clutch, bronze metallic heels and stacked gold bracelets.

"Thank you for being here, and I apologize for keeping you waiting," Alex said, sitting down at the table next to Dahlia.

"We just glad you showed up. But we kept ourselves busy while waiting for your arrival."

"I see. You already got the bubbly flowing. We might as well pour ourselves a glass since we're here to celebrate," Alex grinned.

"Celebrate. That's what we're here for? What we celebrating?"

"I was going to wait until after dinner to make my announcement but we can share the good news now. A month ago I asked Dahlia to be my wife and she accepted. We're getting married."

Dahlia held up her hand, flashing the massive rock on her finger.

"That ring is beautiful," Passion said, practically drooling over the sparkler. That has to be at least ten carats," she continued. It was obvious that Passion wished it were she who was flashing an engagement ring. She turned and looked over at Deion, but he wasn't paying her any attention. He was still processing what Alex said because he was in shock.

"Thank you. Alex has great taste," Dahlia blushed.

"So do you, because what you have on is everything. I saw that exact dress in one of my fashion magazines. Isn't that Gucci?" Reggie's date added.

"Actually Alex picked this out too. It was a gift. He's the best," Dahlia said, giving him a kiss.

"No, you're the best."

"Well, congrats, man." Reggie stood up and gave Alex a hug. "And welcome to the fam," he said, hugging Dahlia too.

"Alex, can I talk to you for a minute, outside?"

"Sure. Dahlia, I'll be right back," Alex said, before following Deion outside. "So what's up, man? You wanted to tell me congratulations in private?"

"No, I wanted to ask you what the fuck are you thinking?"

"Excuse me?"

"Man, you don't even know this broad. How can you even think about marrying her?"

"Deion, I'm not doing this wit' you tonight."

"Doing what...having a real fuckin' conversation? You've known this broad for all of a minute and now you making her yo' wife. What's really going on wit' you?"

"First of all, stop callin' her broad. Her name is Dahlia and she's my fiancé. Secondly, this is my life. I don't have to explain shit to you. This is the woman I want to marry and spend the rest of my life with. If you don't like it then that's your fuckin' problem."

"So our friendship means nothin' to you? You let this broad come in..."

"Didn't I say stop calling her broad?" Alex barked, lounging at Deion. The men were about to brawl until Reggie came out and broke the men apart.

"What the fuck is you guys doing?"

"Instead of this motherfucker being happy for me, he out here talkin' shit about my engagement."

Reggie looked over at Deion who had his face all frowned up still pissed the fuck off. He was waiting for Deion to explain himself, but he said nothing.

"Can you both calm down and come back inside? The ladies are in there waiting for us. The waitress needs to take our orders so we need to bring this party inside the restaurant."

"You all can order whatever you want but I'm done here."

"Alex, don't leave. We supposed to be celebrating." Alex ignored Reggie's pleas and went back inside to get Dahlia so they could leave. "Deion, why the fuck you ruin that man's night?"

"I'm tryna save his life. That woman got Alex fooled. She ain't no good. She playin' that sweet role but I guarantee you she's just a typical scheming-ass gold digger."

"Even if you right, Alex a grown man and talkin' shit about his fiancé is only going to create bad blood. You all have been friends for too long to let that happen. If you don't stop you're going to lose your partner and best friend," Reggie warned.

Chapter 22
No Heart No Love

"I'm glad you called," Alex said, letting Deion in.

"I would've called sooner but I figured you wasn't ready to fuck wit' me yet."

"You figured right, but I've cooled down."

"I fucked up. I was wrong for how I acted that night."

"I know how hard it is for you to admit you're wrong, so thanks, bro."

"I'm just glad we can put this behind us and focus on business. No matter what, we can't let nothin' come between us gettin' this money."

"Speaking of business, there was something I wanted to discuss wit' you."

"Speak. What, you ready to do some more expanding on our drug distribution?"

"None of that. I'm entering a new chapter in my life with Dahlia and I'm leaving the game behind. I'm done."

"Alex, I'm accepting this whole marriage thing, now you're tellin' me I have to accept you giving up the game? We came into this shit together, I thought we was gon' leave it together too."

"We've both made millions from this shit; you're more than welcome to join me in retiring from this game. Real estate investments is going well for me and now that I'm done wit' drugs I'm going even harder. Join me."

"This is what I do. I'm a drug dealer. I hustle for a living and you know what...I enjoy this shit. I thought you did too. Unless you're doing this for your new fiancé."

"Don't blame Dahlia for this, it's my choice. I can't lie, I did enjoy hustling and the sense of power that came with it, but I'm ready to move on while I'm ahead."

"I feel you. Well let me get outta here. I got a bunch of shit to take care of today."

"Cool, don't be a stranger. Although I'll soon be a married man we're still best friends."

"You right, and best friends look out for each other. Talk to you later." Deion left Alex's crib straight plotting. "Tommy, what up. I need to meet wit' you in the next hour and I want you to bring me something..."

"Baby, what time are you coming over tonight? I have a surprise for you," Dahlia said, holding her positive pregnancy test.

"I have a surprise for you too."

"Tell me. What is it?"

"You tell me yours I'll tell you mine."

"Okay, but you go first."

"I'm about to go meet with Danny."

"The man that does some real estate business for you...right?"

"Yep. But I'm meeting with him to close on our new mansion."

"Stop playing!"

"Remember that house I took you to a few weeks ago and said it was the mansion a friend of mine was buying?"

"Ohmigoodness, not that European estate in Buckhead on Crest Valley Road?"

"That would be the house." Dahlia started screaming in the phone and all Alex could do was laugh. "Can you calm down so you can tell me what your surprise is?"

"We're having a baby. I just took the pregnancy test and it came out positive."

"I bet it happened that night I proposed to you in Miami."

"I was thinking the exact same thing."

"Baby, you've just made the happiest man on earth. I never thought I could love you more than I did before but I do. You and this baby are my everything."

"I love you so much too. Please hurry over, I need to be with you."

"I'll be there as soon as I finish things up with Danny. I love you."

"I love you too." When Dahlia was hanging up with Alex she heard someone knocking on her front door. She thought it was the apartment super coming to check on the heater problem she had complained about, but when she opened the door it was Deion. "What are you doing here?"

"I came to apologize to you. Can I come in?"

"Sure." Dahlia was reluctant about talking to Deion but he was Alex's best friend and she did want to get along with him if possible.

"I'm shocked Alex still has you living in this

piece of shit of an apartment. I mean, you are now his fiancé."

"That doesn't sound like an apology to me, but since you're so concerned about my living arrangements, Alex is about to close on a mansion for us in Buckhead."

"I have to give it to you, you're much more than a pretty face. You're very smart. A lot smarter than I gave you credit for."

"What is that supposed to mean?"

"You have this good girl act down to a science. You went from waiting tables, driving a broke-down raggedy car, wearing cheap clothes and living in this dump to a major come up. I applaud you," Deion taunted, clapping his hands.

"I think it's time for you to go," Dahlia said, opening the door.

"I'm not going anywhere," Deion shot back, slamming the door close. "You think you can come in and in a matter of months destroy everything Alex and I have built."

"I'm not trying to destroy anything. Alex and I are in love and we're getting married. Deal with it, Deion, because those are the facts."

"That's where you're wrong." Before Dahlia could blink, Deion had her pinned down to the floor, his hand covering her mouth. See, you should've chosen me and maybe things could've turned out differently for you.

Tears swelled up in Dahlia's eyes when she saw Deion pulling down his pants. She began moving her body violently trying to break free but her petite size was no match for Deion's strength. Dahlia closed her eyes wanting to escape her torture as Deion pounded inside of her. Tears continued to flow down her face as she prayed to God to make this nightmare end. When Deion was finally finished raping her, Dahlia curled up, rocking back and forth.

"Please leave," she mumbled through tears.

"If only it was that easy."

"It is. I won't say anything to Alex. I just want you to go. Please just go."

"I can't do that." Without giving it a second thought, Deion pulled out his gun with the silencer and but two bullets in Dahlia, killing her instantly. Deion then pulled out the baggie of drugs that he'd gotten from Tommy. It had the GMC logo on it. He left it right next to Dahlia's lifeless body before making his exit.

Alex arrived at Dahlia's apartment with

flowers, stuffed animals and a diamond bracelet he'd bought for her at the last minute. They had so much to celebrate. An upcoming wedding, a new home and most importantly, their child. Alex couldn't imagine his life getting any better than it was now.

He knocked on the door but there was no answer. Alex knocked a few more times before using the key he had.

"Maybe she's in the shower and didn't hear me knocking," he said, thinking out loud. But within a few seconds Alex realized that wasn't the case at all. He saw Dahlia's dead, naked body lying on the floor. "Dear God, noooooooooo," Alex wailed, dropping everything out of his hands and cradling Dahlia's limp body. For the next few minutes Alex couldn't take his eyes off of Dahlia until he noticed the baggie of drugs with the GMC logo on it.

His unconceivable pain then turned to full-fledged rage. "These niggas took my wife and my child. They'll pay for this shit...all of them," Alex promised as he continued to hold Dahlia's dead body in his arms.

Chapter 23
WICKED GAMES

Alex woke up in a pool of sweat, huffing and puffing. He couldn't seem to escape the nightmare of finding Dahlia dead. The scene constantly haunted him in his sleep, and Alex felt until he wiped out the entire crew whom he believed to be responsible for her death, this would be his existence.

Alex headed to the bathroom to take a shower, hoping the hot water would somehow cleanse his mind and body of the hell he was living in. When he stood up, Alex noticed he had several missed calls on his cell phone and they were all from Deion. He immediately called him back, wanting to make sure no bullshit was going down.

"What up?"

"Man, I been calling you nonstop."

"I was knocked out. Is everything cool?"

"I got some news on those boys. By Friday we should be able to make our move. You feel me?" Although Deion wasn't giving specifics, Alex knew exactly what he was talking about.

"I sure do. Let's meet tomorrow so I can get the details."

"Cool. See you then."

When Alex hung up with Deion, for the first time in weeks he felt there was a chance he might get some sort of closure. He knew the shit would be on his mind all night, so instead of going to take a shower, Alex got dressed and headed downstairs to the building's 24-hour gym.

"What Alex say?" Reggie asked, finishing up his drink.

"He want us to meet tomorrow."

"Man, I hope that GMC info is legit 'cause them niggas gotta go. What they did to Alex's girl was the ultimate disrespect. They crossed the fuckin' line," Reggie spit.

"You right. But Alex will get the last laugh."

"There ain't nothin' humorous about none of this shit. That nigga lost his wife."

"You know I didn't mean it like that, plus that wasn't his wife."

"They were engaged. Same fuckin' thing, and she was carrying his seed," Reggie said, frowning up at Deion.

"Nah, married and engaged ain't the same fuckin' thing. But why we still talkin' about that shit...she dead and them GMC boys will be dealt with. End of story."

"You a cold nigga. That woman's body barely cold and Alex over there sick, so this ain't hardly the end of nobody story. I just hope our man will be able to move on from this."

"Listen, Alex know how this game go," Deion stated, standing up from the sofa and standing in front of his fireplace with a bottle of Rey Sol Anejo in his hand. "Women are a liability. I feel for Alex. I know his heart hurtin' right now, but he strong. Once he gets revenge, he'll recover and move on. Dahlia will be a distant memory."

Deion was sitting on the bench at Piedmont Park watching kids play on a brisk November day. He thought back to when he and Alex were small boys living in the projects, staying in trouble. Back then their trouble was fun and harmless, now it was costing innocent people their lives.

"What's good, my dude?" Tommy walked up on Deion and said, snapping him out of his thoughts.

"You tell me," Deion replied, before pounding fist with Tommy.

"Same bullshit, just another day. I'm still waiting on you to hit me up wit' some more of that heroin with that extra discount you promised."

"I got you, nigga."

"Cool, but when? You know I'm tryna break free from GMC and get my money up so I can make my own moves."

"I know what the plan is and we gon' make it happen. But we have to watch how we move. You know I had to kill my partner's woman because I found out she was snitching to the Feds. So I was just trying to let things die down a little. But I think things are good now. Plus, we want to make sure the shit is done right and your boys don't start thinking you up to something."

"I feel you, but fuck them. I'm tryna eat good like the rest of them niggas. They want me to be a worker forever and never a boss."

Deion listened to Tommy complain, trying

to keep his patience. All he really wanted to do was confirm the location where the GMC meeting was supposed to be Friday night without arousing suspicion from Tommy. Deion knew Tommy was ready to start running his own shit but he wasn't prepared to see his crew murdered in the process, so Deion had to proceed with caution.

"I have to go out of town later on today but I'll be back Friday. How 'bout we meet up Friday night and I hook you up?"

"Bet, my man." Tommy started smiling hard as hell at what Deion had just told him. "But can it be early Friday, 'cause we have a GMC meeting Friday night and that shit mandatory"

"Nigga, you was just sayin' fuck them, now you worried 'bout makin' mandatory meetings," Deion said, clowning Tommy.

"I know...I know. But until you hit me off a few more times and my money right, I gotta keep fuckin' wit' them niggas."

"I feel you, but I can't make it early Friday. I won't be back in town until later that night. Where is your meeting? I can hook up wit' you right afterwards."

"The Fire and Ice Lounge."

"I know exactly where that is. So what time is

the meeting?"

"It starts at nine but I'ma try to break out early so we can meet up."

"How long the meeting normally last?"

"Couple hours. Then niggas just be drinkin', eatin' and kickin' it."

"So what time you gon' try to break out?"

"Damn, I just remembered that Carlos need me to go pick up some money for him Friday so I won't be at the meeting. I'll probably get back late so can we meet up Saturday instead."

"That's even better," Deion said, grinning inside. Deion didn't want Tommy to be there when they hit up his crew because he still planned on utilizing him for some other shit. Deion could tell Tommy was the type of dude that would be down to do just about whatever he asked. Now, there would be no headache of trying to figure out a way to get Tommy away from the lounge before they swarmed the spot.

"Good deal. So I'll see you Saturday for sure. The earlier the better, 'cause I'm tryna make that chicken."

"I hear you. I'll have that heroin to you first thing Saturday morning."

"Appreciate it. See you then," Tommy said,

shaking Deion's hand before walking off.

Deion stood with satisfaction as he envisioned his plan unfolding correctly. In just a couple of days he would be gaining even more power on the streets and resolving some problems that needed to be put to rest. With the GMC members dead, Deion would be able to supply the majority of their customers, which equated to a major boost in revenue. Not only that, Alex would finally get retribution for Dahlia's death and put that shit behind him once and for all.

Alex could never find out that it was him that raped and killed his fiancé. Deion knew that was the one sin Alex would not ever forgive him for and it would be the end to not only their partnership but also friendship. He refused to let that happen. Deion had convinced himself that Dahlia was better off dead because she was coming between the lifelong best friends, and that what he did to her was justified. As Deion stared out at the children playing in the park one last time, he vowed no one would come between him and Alex ever again.

Chapter 24
STICK TO THE SCRIPT

"So you sure that meeting is going down tomorrow night?"

"Positive. My inside connect confirmed the time and location."

"If he's down with GMC, how do you know it's not a setup?"

"The dude has no idea that we're taking down the entire crew. He gave me the info on some casual shit. He mentioned it to me a few weeks ago and yesterday he confirmed that it's still a go."

"I wish I could personally put a bullet in each of those niggas myself," Alex said, walking over to a picture of Dahlia that he still kept on a table in the living room. He picked up the frame and stared at it for what felt like an eternity to Deion.

"I got everybody lined up. We going in there deep. Not one member of the Get Money Crew is gonna make it out of that lounge alive," Deion stated, wanting Alex to snap out of that trance he was in. "We all meeting up at our warehouse tomorrow night at eight, then we head to Fire and Ice. You'll be ready... right?" Alex didn't say a word. He was completely engrossed in his own thoughts and he hadn't even heard what Deion had said. "Yo, Alex. You gon' be there right?" he asked in a louder tone.

"Be where?" Alex finally said as if in a slight daze.

"Man, I know you going through a hard time but it's time to let this shit go. You not even focusing."

"How the fuck can I focus on anything right now?"

"You about to get revenge on the niggas responsible for this shit, what else do you want?"

"I want my woman back. I want the child we were supposed to have together. Can you give me that?" Deion could not only hear the rage in Alex's voice but he could see it in every muscle in his face and body.

"No I can't, but I can give you the next best thing...those niggas' blood on your hands. I promised you that we would get retribution and I'm delivering on that promise."

"And I love you for that, Deion. You're my brother. You've held it down in every way since this shit went down and I'll always be grateful to you for that. Thank you."

"You don't have to thank me...we family. You always have my back and I'll always have yours. It's nothing but love between us," Deion said, giving Alex a brotherly hug.

"Listen, I gotta go handle some business wit' some people but don't forget, tomorrow night at eight we all meeting at our warehouse."

"I'll be there. I'm ready for this shit to be over with."

"Cool, but we'll speak later on," Deion said before heading out.

Before Deion even reached his car, he heard a text message come through and saw that it was from Alex. It simply said, *Thank You Bro*. Deion smiled. For the last year, because of their different views on business, unnecessary deaths and other bullshit Alex and Deion's relationship had seemed to be crumbling. Their once unbreakable bond was showing signs of discord. But since Dahlia's death, the two men seemed closer than ever. Deion figured a big part of it was due to them coming together to seek retaliation for Dahlia's murder. Of course, it was based on all lies, but that didn't bother Deion in the least. As he thought about how all this would be over tomorrow night, he noticed Passion was calling him.

"Hey baby, what's up?"

"Deion, there is some dude following me."

"What you mean following...like a stalker?" he asked, hearing the panic in Passion's voice.

"I don't think he's no stalker. I mean, I don't recognize his face and I haven't worked at the club in months."

"Where you at now?"

"At home."

"Okay, I'm on my way over." When Deion hung up with Passion he called Popcorn to let him know he would be a little late meeting with him.

"I was just about to call you," Popcorn said as soon as he answered the phone.

"Why is there a problem?"

"Not sure. I've seen this car a couple times in front of my apartment today. When I was about to leave to come meet you, I looked out my window and saw it again. It could be nothing, 'cause mad motherfuckers be over here, but something don't feel right."

"That's crazy, 'cause Passion just called me saying she thought somebody was following her."

"Oh shit."

"Exactly. This shit can't be no coincidence. I'm about to go over to see Passion now and check things out. Have you left your crib yet?"

"Nope. I called you right after I looked out the window and seen the car again."

"Cool. Stay there until I'm done wit' Passion. Do you think whoever it is would come up in your spot?"

"They can play wit' they life if they want to 'cause I'm armed and ready."

"I know you are," Deion laughed. "I'll hit you when I finish up with Passion and let you know how we gon' do."

When Deion arrived at Passion's townhouse he noticed her BMW parked out front but no suspicious cars. Instead of pulling right beside her crib, he decided to park across the street. Just in case somebody was planning a drive-by they wouldn't know he was there. As Deion started walking towards her place, he dialed her cell but she didn't answer. He tried two more times before deciding to try her at home. Right when Deion was about to call the landline, what sounded like a sonic boom jerked his body in the air, sending him crashing to the ground.

Deion could see windows being blown out and glass shattering from Passion's townhouse. The sudden violent burst of energy had Deion's ears piercing, body numb and head throbbing. His eyes could barely focus, but he could see that the engulfed flames were swallowing Passion's townhouse. Deion attempted to go towards the home to see if Passion was inside so he could help her escape, but a second explosion went off, making that impossible. Whoever was inside was dead and there was no saving them. Deion thought about Passion and her son and all he could do was shake his head. Deion had to practically drag himself to his car, and once inside the next thing he did was call Popcorn.

"Everything good?" Popcorn asked when he answered the phone.

"Nah, ain't nothin' good right now."

"What happened?"

"Passion's crib just blew the fuck up."

"Are you serious? Was she inside?"

"Yeah I think so. I think her lil' man was inside too. Her car was parked out front and she knew I was on my way over. This shit crazy. I ain't never seen a building just blow up like that."

"Fuck! Who you think behind this shit?"

"Hell if I know. I done fucked over so many motherfuckers it could be any damn body."

"We need to figure this shit out before things get any worse."

"I agree. Have you seen that car again?"

"Nah, not since the last time I spoke to you."

"So do you want me to meet you at your crib or do you want to meet someplace else?"

"I'll come to you. I ain't feeling too good about staying up in here."

"I feel you. Where you wanna meet?"

"Umm, let's meet at that...what the..." those were the last words Deion heard Popcorn say before a loud *Pow...Pow...Pow* rang out and then what sounded like the phone dropping to the floor.

"Hello! Hello!" Deion screamed through his cell, but there was dead silence for a few seconds until he heard a deep, raspy voice say.

"Nigga, you next," before the phone went dead. Deion leaned back in his car seat and closed his eyes. At that moment he couldn't fathom shit getting any worse.

Chapter 25
FLESH OF MY FLESH, BLOOD OF MY BLOOD

"Thanks for coming to pick me up," Deion said, when he got in on the passenger side of Alex's Range Rover.

"This ain't nothin'. We headed to the same spot anyway. I was a little surprised when you asked me to pick you up since you don't like to wait around on nobody for a ride," Alex joked.

"True, but I wanted us to have some time to talk in private before we got to the warehouse."

"What's wrong, is there a problem?"

Deion let out a deep sigh before answering. "Man, a problem don't begin to describe what the fuck is going on right now."

"Do I need to pull over?" Alex asked, observing the seriousness on Deion's face.

"No, keep driving. So much done got fucked

up, I at least want this shit to go down correctly tonight."

"Talk to me."

"Both Passion and Popcorn got killed yesterday. I think her son might be dead too."

"You have to be fuckin' kiddin' me! What the fuck happened?"

"Passion called me yesterday after I left your crib saying she thought somebody was following her. On my way to her spot, I called Popcorn to let him know I would running late to met him and he tells me he think somebody been driving past his apartment watching him too."

"That definitely wasn't no coincidence."

"Exactly. So I tell him to hold tight until after I check on Passion. When I get to her crib that shit blow the fuck up."

"What you mean, like a bomb or some shit?"

"Yeah, her shit just exploded. I been watching the news and they mentioned the explosion but haven't identified the bodies yet."

"Yo, that shit is fucked up. I'm sorry man. I know you been dealing with Passion for a minute now."

"Yeah, that shit do hurt. And what make it even more fucked up is that Passion and maybe even her son is dead because she fuckin' wit' me. Then Popcorn too."

"So what happened to him?"

"After I see Passion's crib blow the fuck up, I get in my car and call Popcorn and let him know what happen. I asked him if the car was still driving past his apartment and he told me no. So he's on his way to come meet me and next thing I hear is gunshots blasting in the background. Then some motherfucker get on the phone and say I'm next."

"Yo, this shit is just going from bad to worse. I bet you those GMC niggas behind this shit. First they fuck me over and take Dahlia out my life, now they fuckin' wit you. Them niggas need to be stopped, and after tonight they reign will finally be over."

Deion just nodded his head, agreeing with what Alex said. But he was almost a hundred percent sure that them GMC boys had nothing to do with what happened to Passion or Popcorn. Deion had Alex blaming GMC for everything fucked up going on in their lives, but in all actuality them niggas was only out here trying to get money just like them. They were an easy mark for Deion to pin everything so he was riding the shit out. But now with this new shit popping off, Deion had to figure out who was trying to bring him down. Deion had no intentions of dying, so that meant he had to murder his enemies before they had a chance to put him six feet under.

"No worries, them niggas will be dealt with," Deion said, cosigning with Alex.

"You damn right. There's 'bout to be a lot of slow singin' and flower bringin' in the ATL, courtesy of me. Let's do this shit so I can finally have a fuckin' good night sleep," Alex stated as he pulled up his car in the parking lot in front of their warehouse.

"I see everybody on time," Deion commented, looking at all the cars out front.

"Good. That means motherfuckers ready for war."

When Alex and Deion entered the warehouse there were at least a dozen men dressed in black, wearing bulletproof vests, just in case GMC was able to bust off too. There were piles of guns stacked on a center table and Alex was anxious to get his hands on them.

"Everybody ready?" Deion asked, knowing by the looks of the men that they were waiting on them.

"We been ready," most of the men said in unison. Deion locked eyes with each man and all he saw was death. But that's why he used them. They were born killers. Each of them had proven that when they took down Jose's crew; now they would do the same with GMC. Not wanting to hold things up, Alex and Deion put on their bulletproof vests, and each grabbed an AK-47 and a Twin .45 before making their exit.

Before the three black tinted vans pulled up to Fire and Ice, one of the men drove around the parking lot first to check everything out. They wanted to make sure that GMC didn't have men patrolling the area since their monthly meeting was taking place. Once they were given the go, they parked the vans and the men stormed the lounge with guns blazing. With Alex and Deion's crew sneaking up on the GMC members, they didn't stand a chance against their attack.

The men were gathered on the lower level, sitting on couches by the bar. Without warning, gunfire ripped through the lounge, easily striking the intended targets. The white couches quickly turned blood red as bullets tore open skin, leaving dead bodies slumped over on the floor. Some of the Get Money Crew tried to reach for their guns or make a run for it in an attempt to avoid the hot lead balls being fired in their direction, but it was all in vain. Alex and Deion's men were rolling too deep, especially since the other side was completely unprepared. One of the men tried to use a dead body as a shield but Alex was relentless in his pursuit. He walked right up on him and emptied his entire clip in the man's face and body. He quickly reloaded and tracked down his next prey.

Through what felt like an eternity but was actually only a few minutes, they had basically slaughtered almost forty men. There was complete silence except for the sounds of gunshots during that duration of time, and as quickly as it had started, it was over.

"Let's go," Deion said, nodding his head in the direction of the exit door.

As the men were heading out, Alex stopped dead in his tracks. Deion was already by the door, so Alex put his index finger to his mouth, motioning Deion to be quiet. He listened intently, trying to figure out where the noise was coming from. He spun around and saw what appeared to be somebody balled up under one of the chairs. There was a dead body somewhat blocking the angle but Alex thought he saw a finger move. He walked over to the location with his gun aimed. Alex kicked the dead body to the side and saw a man balled up in the fetal position.

"Please don't kill me," he begged, with tears rolling down his face. The man was breathing hard and as he tried to calm down he recognized Alex's face. "Man, you Deion partner, why would you do this?" he asked with confusion in his voice.

"Nigga, do you even have to ask that dumb fuckin' question! This is payback for you bitch-ass niggas murdering my fiancé and unborn child for no fuckin' reason. Now all you niggas gon' die," Alex barked, ready to pull the trigger.

"What the fuck! GMC ain't had nothin' to do wit' yo' fiancé death. You shootin' at the wrong motherfuckers. I can tell you exactly who killed yo' girl. Your...," before he could get out another word, Deion walked up and put a hollow tip bullet through Tommy's neck and right eye.

Nigga, you was not supposed to be here. I had plans for you too, but there was no way I could let you tell Alex that it was me and not your crew that murdered Dahlia. You shoulda took yo' ass to Nashville, Deion thought to himself after killing Tommy.

"Why did you shoot him?"

"What you mean? Everybody had to die. We ain't leaving no witnesses," Deion shot back.

"But he was about to tell me something."

"Tell you what?"

"He was about to tell me who killed Dahlia."

"Nigga, look around. You see all these dead bodies. We know exactly who killed her. You had a gun to that man's head. Of course he gon' tell you it wasn't them. Now let's get the fuck outta here. I'm sure somebody done called the police by now." Alex still wasn't moving. "Let's go!" Deion screamed out again, and this time Alex listened.

Later on that night as Alex lay on his bed staring up at the ceiling, that good night's sleep he was hoping for never came. He thought after getting retribution for Dahlia that his mind would finally find some peace, but instead he kept replaying what Tommy said to him before he died.

Could it be possible that GMC didn't have anything to do with Dahlia's death? Could we have killed all those men for no reason? But it had to be them. They left a baggie of their drugs by Dahlia's body as if to taunt me, Alex thought to himself.

"Let me stop thinking about this bullshit. Deion was right. If a nigga got a gun to your head, you'll say anything if you think it will keep you alive," Alex stated out loud, wanting to put an end to all the second guessing. Alex reached over to turn off the light on his nightstand and saw a private number pop up on his phone. At first he wasn't going to answer but with it being so late, he was curious to know who was calling.

"Hello."

"Listen carefully. If you want to know who killed your fiancé, meet me tomorrow and I'll let you know what really happened."

"Who is this?"

"Think about what I said. I'll call you back tomorrow. If you want to know the truth then you'll meet with me."

The phone went dead and Alex felt numbness in the pit of his stomach. He didn't know what the fuck was going on but he planned on meeting the person tomorrow. If there were somebody else who was responsible for Dahlia's death, then their blood would be on his hands too.

Deion had a bottle of liquor in one hand and the remote to the television in the other. He sat in his bed scrolling through channels, thinking about bullshit that had gone down the last few days. The only positive he could come up with was that they were able to get rid of every member of the Get Money Crew. Initially, Deion regretted that he'd had to kill Tommy, but the more he thought about it, he figured it was for the best. He didn't need anybody else walking the streets privy to the truth. The only other person who knew how Dahlia died was now dead and Deion would take the secret to his grave.

Ring...Ring...Ring...

Deion glanced over at his cell and answered without even seeing who was calling. "Yo," Deion said, feeling halfway sleepy and halfway drunk.

"Uncle Deion, it's me, Demonte." Hearing Demonte's voice sounding full of fear made Deion focus.

"Demonte, is that you? Where you at?"

"They took us. The man has me and Mommy. He said he is going to kill us unless you do what he say."

"What man, and where are you?" Demonte didn't answer, instead another voice got on the phone. It sounded like the same man that told him he was next after killing Popcorn.

"You want to see yo' girl and her son again, then you better come up wit' this chicken. If not, they'll wish they had died in that explosion."

"Nigga, how much you want?"

"Just make sure you keep answering yo' phone. I'll be in touch to let you know."

"Let me speak..." Before Deion could finish his sentence the man hung up. He threw his phone down on the floor in frustration. He didn't like how any of this shit was going down. He also wondered if Passion and Demonte hadn't died in that explosion, then who had?

Deion didn't appreciate the fact that someone was trying to squeeze money from him, especially using a child to do so. If Passion was the only victim involved, more than likely Deion would've said he wasn't giving him a penny. It was because he did have a soft spot for kids that Deion was even considering paying up. But that would all depend on how much the kidnapper was asking for. The price of the ransom would be the determining factor on whether he would save Passion and her son's life. With that, Deion closed his eyes and went to sleep.

NO ONE MAN SHOULD HAVE ALL THAT POWER...BUT THERE WERE TWO

Now Available!

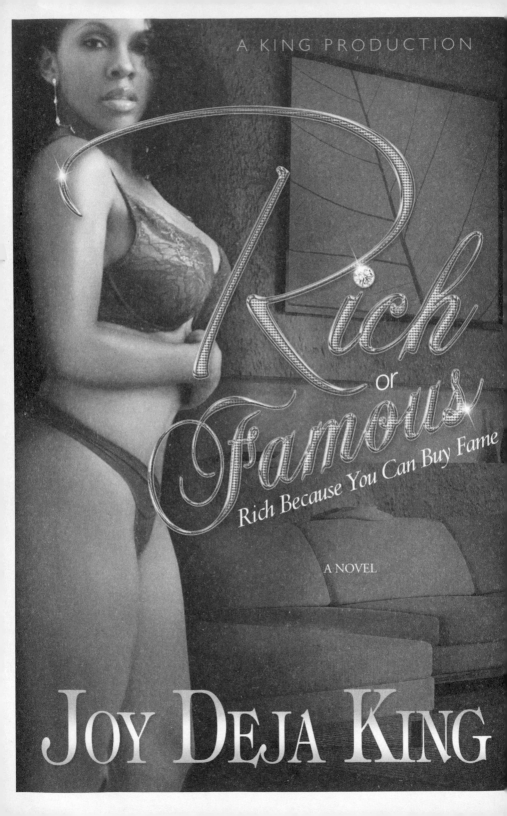

A KING PRODUCTION

Rich
or
Famous

Rich Because You Can Buy Fame

A NOVEL

JOY DEJA KING

Lorenzo

Welcome To My World

Before I die, if you don't remember anything else I ever taught you, know this. A man will be judged, not on what he has but how much of it. So you find a way to make money and when you think you've made enough, make some more, because you'll need it to survive in this cruel world. Money will be the only thing to save you. As I sat across from Darnell those words my father said to me on his deathbed played in my head.

"Yo, Lorenzo, are you listening to me, did you hear anything I said?"

"I heard everything you said. The problem for you is I don't give a fuck." I responded, giving a casual shoulder shrug as I rested my thumb under my chin with my index finger above my mouth.

"What you mean, you don't give a fuck? We been doing business for over three years now and that's the best you got for me?"

"Here's the thing, Darnell, I got informants all over these streets. As a matter of fact that broad you've had in your back pocket for the last few weeks is one of them."

"I don't understand what you saying," Darnell said swallowing hard. He tried to keep the tone of his voice calm, but his body composure was speaking something different.

"Alexus, has earned every dollar I've paid her to fuck wit' yo' blood suckin' ass. You a fake fuck wit' no fangs. You wanna play wit' my 100 g's like you at the casino. That's a real dummy move, Darnell." I could see the sweat beads gathering, resting in the creases of Darnell's forehead.

"Lorenzo, man, I don't know what that bitch told you but none of it is true! I swear 'bout four niggas ran up in my crib last night and took all my shit. Now that I think about it, that trifling ho Alexus probably had me set up! She fucked us both over!"

I shook my head for a few seconds not believing this muthafucker was saying that shit with a straight face. "I thought you said it was two niggas that ran up in your crib now that shit done doubled. Next thing you gon' spit is that all of Marcy projects was in on the stickup."

"Man, I can get your money. I can have it to

you first thing tomorrow. I swear!"

"The thing is I need my money right now." I casually stood up from my seat and walked towards Darnell who now looked like he had been dipped in water. Watching him fall apart in front of my eyes made up for the fact that I would never get back a dime of the money he owed me.

"Zo, you so paid, this shit ain't gon' even faze you. All I'm asking for is less than twenty-four hours. You can at least give me that," Darnell pleaded.

"See, that's your first mistake, counting my pockets. My money is *my* money, so yes this shit do faze me."

"I didn't mean it like that. I wasn't tryna disrespect you. By this time tomorrow you will have your money and we can put this shit behind us." Darnell's eyes darted around in every direction instead of looking directly at me. A good liar, he was not.

"Since you were robbed of the money you owe me and the rest of my drugs, how you gon' get me my dough? I mean the way you tell it, they didn't leave you wit' nothin' but yo' dirty draws."

"I'll work it out. Don't even stress yourself, I got you, man."

"What you saying is that the nigga you so called aligned yourself with, by using my money and my product, is going to hand it back over to you?"

"Zo, what you talking 'bout? I ain't aligned

myself wit' nobody. That slaw ass bitch Alexus feeding you lies."

"No, that's you feeding me lies. Why don't you admit you no longer wanted to work for me? You felt you was big shit and could be your own boss. So you used my money and product to buy your way in with this other nigga to step in my territory. But you ain't no boss you a poser. And your need to perpetrate a fraud is going to cost you your life."

"Lorenzo, don't do this man! This is all a big misunderstanding. I swear on my daughter I will have your money tomorrow. Fuck, if you let me leave right now I'll have that shit to you tonight!" I listened to Darnell stutter his words.

My men, who had been patiently waiting in each corner of the warehouse, dressed in all black, loaded with nothing but artillery, stepped out of the darkness ready to obliterate the enemy I had once considered my best worker. Darnell's eyes widened as he witnessed the men who had saved and protected him on numerous occasions, as he dealt with the vultures he encountered in the street life, now ready to end his.

"Don't do this, Zo! Pleeease," Darnell was now on his knees begging.

"Damn, nigga, you already a thief and a backstabber. Don't add, going out crying like a bitch to that too. Man the fuck up. At least take this bullet like a soldier."

"I'm sorry, Zo. Please don't do this. I gotta daughter that need me. Pleeease man, I'll do anything. Just don't kill me." The tears were pouring down Darnell's face and instead of softening me up it just made me even more pissed at his punk ass.

"Save your fuckin' tears. You shoulda thought about your daughter before you stole from me. You're the worse sort of thief. I invite you into my home, I make you a part of my family and you steal from me, you plot against me. Your daughter doesn't need you. You have nothing to teach her."

My men each pulled out their gat ready to attack and I put my hand up motioning them to stop. For the first time since Darnell arrived, a calm gaze spread across his face.

"I knew you didn't have the heart to let them kill me, Zo. We've been through so much together. I mean you Tania's God Father. We bigger than this and we will get through it," Darnell said, halfway smiling as he began getting off his knees and standing up.

"You're right, I don't have the heart to let them kill you, I'ma do that shit myself." Darnell didn't even have a chance to let what I said resonate with him because I just sprayed that muthafucker like the piece of shit he was. "Clean this shit up," I said, stepping over Darnell's bullet ridden body as I made my exit.

Prologue

Lorenzo stepped out of his black Bugatti Coupe and entered the non-descript building in East Harlem. Normally, Lorenzo would have at least one henchman with him, but he wanted complete anonymity. When he made his entrance, the man Lorenzo planned on hiring was patiently waiting.

"I hope you came prepared for what I need."

"I wouldn't have wasted my time if I hadn't," Lorenzo stated before pulling out two pictures from a manila envelope and tossing them on the table.

"This is her?"

"Yes, her name is Alexus. Study this face very carefully, 'cause this is the woman you're going to bring to me, so I can kill."

"Are you sure you don't want me to handle it? Murder is included in my fee."

"I know, but personally killing this backstabbing snake is a gift to myself"

"Who is the other woman?"

"Her name is Lala."

"Do you want her dead, too?"

"I haven't decided. For now, just find her whereabouts and any other pertinent information. She also has a young daughter. I want you to find out how the little girl is doing. That will determine whether Lala lives or dies."

"Is there anybody else on your hit list?"

"This is it for now, but that might change at any moment. Now, get on your job, because I want results ASAP," Lorenzo demanded before tossing stacks of money next to the photos.

"I don't think there's a need to count. I'm sure it's all there," the hit man said, picking up one of the stacks and flipping through the bills.

"No doubt, and you can make even more, depending on how quickly I see results."

"I appreciate the extra incentive."

"It's not for you, it's for me. Everyone that is responsible for me losing the love of my life will pay in blood. The sooner the better."

Lorenzo didn't say another word and instead made his exit. He came and delivered; the rest was up to the hit man he had hired. But Lorenzo wasn't worried, he was just one of the many killers on his payroll hired to do the exact same job. He wanted to guarantee that Alexus was delivered to him alive. In his heart, he not only blamed Alexus and Lala for getting him locked up, but also held both of them responsible for Dior taking her own life. As he sat in his jail cell, Lorenzo promised himself that once he got out, if need be he would spend the rest of his life making sure both women received the ultimate retribution.

A KING PRODUCTION

DRAKE

A NOVEL

JOY DEJA KING
AND CHRIS BOOKER

Prologue

"Push! Push!" the doctor directed Kim, as he held the top of the baby's head, hoping this would be the final push that would bring a new life into the world.

The hospital's delivery room was packed with both Kim and Drake's family, and although the large crowd irritated Drake, he still managed to video record the birth of his son. After four hours of labor, Kim gave birth to a 6.5-pound baby boy, who they already named Derrick Jamal Henson Jr. Drake couldn't help but to shed a few tears of joy, at the new addition to his family, but the harsh reality of his son's safety quickly replaced his joy with anger.

Drake was nobody's angel and beyond his light brown eyes and charming smile, he was one of the most feared men in the City of Philadelphia, due to his street cred. He put a lot of work in on the blocks of South Philly, where he grew up. He mainly pushed drugs and gambled, but from time to time he'd place well-known dealers into the trunk of his car and hold them for ransom, according to how much that person was worth.

"I need everybody to leave the room for awhile." Drake told the people in the hospital room, wanting to share a private moment alone with Kim and his son.

The families took a few minutes saying their

goodbyes, before leaving. Kim and Drake sat alone in the room, rejoicing over the birth of baby Derrick. The only interruption was doctors coming in and out of the room, to check up on the baby, mainly because they were a little concerned about his breathing. The doctor informed Drake that he would run a few more tests, to make sure the baby would be fine.

"So, what are you going to do?" Kim questioned Drake, while he was cradling the baby.

"Do about what?" he shot back, without lifting his head up. Drake knew what Kim was alluding to, but he had no interest in discussing it. Once Kim became pregnant, Drake agreed to leave the street life alone, if not completely then significantly cutting back, after their baby was born. They both feared if he didn't stop living that street life, he would land in the box. Drake felt he and jail were like night and day: they could never be together.

"You know what I'm talking about, Drake. Don't play stupid with me," Kim said, poking him in his head with her forefinger.

He smiled. "I gave you my word I was out of the game when you had our baby. Unless my eyes are deceiving me, I think what I'm holding in my arms is our son. Just give me a couple days to clean up the streets and then we can sit down and come up with a plan on how to invest the money we got."

Cleaning up the streets meant selling all the drugs he had and collecting the paper owed to him from his workers and guys he fronted weight to. All together there was about 100-k due, not to mention the fact he had to appoint someone to take over his bread winning crack houses and street corners that made him millions of dollars.

Drake's thoughts came to a halt when his phone started to ring. Sending the call straight to voicemail didn't help any, because it rang again. Right when he reached to turn the phone off, he noticed it was Peaches calling. If it were anybody else, he probably would've declined, but Peaches wasn't just anybody.

"Yo," he answered, shifting the baby to his other arm, while trying to avoid Kim's eyes cutting over at him.

"He knows! He knows everything!" Peaches yelled, with terror in her voice.

Peaches wasn't getting good reception out in the woods, where Villain had left her for dead, so the words Drake was hearing were broken up. All he understood was, "Villain knows!" That was enough to get his heart racing. His heart wasn't racing out of fear, but rather excitement.

In many ways, Villain and Drake were cut from the same cloth. They even both shared tattoos of several teardrops under their eyes. It seemed like gunplay was the only thing that turned Drake on—besides fucking—and when he could feel it in the air, murder was the only thing on his mind.

Drake hung up the phone and tried to call Peaches back, to see if he could get better reception, but her phone went straight to voicemail. Damn! He thought to himself as he tried to call her back repeatedly and block out Kim's voice as she steadily asked him if everything was alright.

"Drake, what's wrong?"

"Nothing. I gotta go. I'll be back in a couple of hours,"

he said, handing Kim their son.

"How sweet! There's nothing like family!" said a voice coming from the direction of the door.

Not yet lifting his head up from his son to see who had entered the room, at first Drake thought it was a doctor, but once the sound of the familiar voice kicked in, Drake's heart began beating at an even more rapid pace. He turned to see Villain standing in the doorway, chewing on a straw and clutching what appeared to be a gun at his waist. Drake's first instinct was to reach for his own weapon, but remembering that he left it in the car made his insides burn. Surely, if he had his gun on him, there would have been a showdown right there in the hospital.

"Can I come in?" Villain asked, in an arrogant tone, as he made his way over to the visitors' chairs. "Let me start off by saying congratulations on having a bastard child."

Villain's remarks made Drake's jaw flutter continuously from fury. Sensing shit was about to go left, Kim attempted to get out of the bed with her baby to leave the room, but before her feet could hit the floor, Villain pulled out a .50 Caliber Desert Eagle and placed it on his lap. The gun was so enormous that Drake could damn near read off the serial number on the slide. Kim looked at the nurse's button and was tempted to press it.

"Push the button and I'll kill all three of y'all. Scream, and I'ma kill all three of y'all. Bitch," Villian paused, making sure the words sunk in. "if you even blink the wrong way, I'ma kill all three of y'all."

"What the fuck you want?" Drake asked, still trying to be firm in his speech.

"You know, at first, I thought about getting my money back and then killin' you, for setting my brother up wit' those bitches you got working for you. But on my way here I just said, 'Fuck the money!' I just wanna kill the nigga."

Deep down inside, Drake wanted to ask for his life to be spared, but his pride wouldn't allow it. Not even the fact that his newborn son was in the room could make Drake beg to stay alive, which made Villain more eager to lullaby his ass into a permanent sleep.

Villain wanted to see the fear in his eyes before he pulled the trigger, but Drake was a G, and was bound to play that role 'til he kissed death.

Order Form

A King Production
P.O. Box 912
Collierville, TN 38027
www.joydejaking.com
www.twitter.com/joydejaking

Name: _____

Address: _____

City/State: _____

Zip: _____

QUANTITY	TITLES	PRICE	TOTAL
_____	Bitch	$15.00	_____
_____	Bitch Reloaded	$15.00	_____
_____	The Bitch Is Back	$15.00	_____
_____	Queen Bitch	$15.00	_____
_____	Last Bitch Standing	$15.00	_____
_____	Superstar	$15.00	_____
_____	Ride Wit' Me	$12.00	_____
_____	Stackin' Paper	$15.00	_____
_____	Trife Life To Lavish	$15.00	_____
_____	Trife Life To Lavish II	$15.00	_____
_____	Stackin' Paper II	$15.00	_____
_____	Rich or Famous	$15.00	_____
_____	Rich or Famous Part 2	$15.00	_____
_____	Bitch A New Beginning	$15.00	_____
_____	Mafia Princess Part 1	$15.00	_____
_____	Mafia Princess Part 2	$15.00	_____
_____	Mafia Princess Part 3	$15.00	_____
_____	Mafia Princess Part 4	$15.00	_____
_____	Boss Bitch	$15.00	_____
_____	Baller Bitches Vol. 1	$15.00	_____
_____	Baller Bitches Vol. 2	$15.00	_____
_____	Bad Bitch	$15.00	_____
_____	Still The Baddest Bitch	$15.00	_____
_____	Power	$15.00	_____
_____	Power 2	$15.00	_____
_____	Princess Fever "Birthday Bash"	$9.99	_____

Shipping/Handling (Via Priority Mail) $6.50 1-2 Books, $8.95 3-4 Books add $1.95 for ea. Additional book.

Total: $_____ FORMS OF ACCEPTED PAYMENTS: Certified or government issued checks and money Orders, all mail in orders take 5-7 Business days to be delivered